It was 1.15 a.m. when she was awakened roughly and dragged from her bed. Half asleep, she stumbled down the corridor, forced through the dim light by the strong hands of two burly uniformed soldiers. They manhandled her, not even giving her time to catch her breath before pushing her through a doorway and down a narrow staircase into a dingy grey cellar. A single, dazzlingly strong light glared at her from its position on a bare wooden table-top in the centre of the room. Liz blinked and staggered slightly as she was released. Her hands went up automatically to rub her upper arms where red marks stood out on the white flesh.

It was the moment all the recruits dreaded, the mock interrogation which could happen to any of them at any stage of their training, at any time of the day or night.

WISH ME LUCK

by Rachel Silver

ARROW BOOKS

Arrow Books Limited
62-65 Chandos Place, London WC2N 4NW

An imprint of Century Hutchinson Limited

London Melbourne Sydney Auckland
Johannesburg and agencies throughout
the world

First published 1988

© LWT 1987

Printed and bound in Great Britain by
Anchor Brendon Limited, Tiptree, Essex

ISBN 0 09 958450 6

Suzanna Hamilton as Matty Firman
Kate Buffery as Liz Grainger
Julian Glover as Colonel Cadogan
Jane Asher as Faith Ashley
Series created by Lavinia Warner and Jill Hyem
Written by Jill Hyem, Kevin Clarke and Colin Shindler
Producers: Colin Shindler and Lavinia Warner
Executive Producer: Nick Elliott
Director: Gordon Flemyng

For my son Benjamin Amarnath Silver

CHAPTER 1

Cairo
16 March 1942

My darling Liz,

How are you and Vicky and Evelyn?

Here in Cairo it is very hot; my office is stifling and I am forever filling out forms and shuffling pieces of paper. It's not much of a life for a soldier!

My darling how I miss you! I think of you and Vicky all the time. You ask me what my life is like here. Perhaps you have some romantic image of my dwelling near the Pyramids? Not so at all; I live on the British compound in a bungalow more suited to Bognor than the Middle East and hear the accents of Yorkshire and Glasgow under my windows each morning. Unlike Lawrence of Arabia, I have no proud dark-skinned servant; my batman is a sour-tempered postman from Huddersfield!

What I would give to see some real action. My darling wife, perhaps even from so far away you will be able to sympathize with me when I say I would like to be transferred to an active fighting unit. I feel the real war is passing me by.

One of the things that keeps me going is thinking of you safely going on with our life far from the London bombs. Whenever I want to throw it all up, I think of you calmly bringing up our little daughter in the Devon countryside where you grew up.

Sometimes I wake up in the night and wonder what you are doing at that moment. Please write and tell me more about Vicky's progress, I feel I'm missing her childhood. Thank her for the splendid drawing and give her a big kiss from me. Send my best wishes to your mother.

Your affectionate husband,
Laurence

It was drizzling at Northover Grange – a large, red-brick, eighteenth-century mock-Gothic mansion partly overgrown with ivy and wisteria. Inside the bay-windowed library, Liz screwed up the letter in her hand and with a rush of irritation flung it into the wastepaper basket under her writing desk. It was all very well for him to think *he* was leading a frustrated existence, but in the next breath he was happily thinking of her cloistered in Devon with her mother and Vicky.

Sitting at the mahogany writing desk where her father had often sat before her, Liz tried to master the unreasonable irritation aroused in her by her husband's letter. She just could not believe that he could be so blind to the frustrations of her present way of life. Now she was back in Devon, she realized how much the years at the Sorbonne in Paris and her married life in their Knightsbridge flat had meant to her. She could not be happy with the simple domesticity of country life; watching Vicky develop was not enough. She missed the interest of hearing about Laurence's cases and his work as a barrister; their evenings out together dining and seeing a show; their cluster of interesting friends and acquaintances.

It was no wonder Laurence had no time to think of her troubles, she told herself firmly; he was fighting a war. Perhaps she was letting herself become selfish. She must be practical – her war work was Vicky. On that thought, she got up and strode across the faded Persian carpet and determinedly entered the hall.

'Vicky, time for a walk. Mummy, are you coming?' she called up the stairs. Standing in the hall, Liz, at twenty-seven, looked tall and graceful, her fair hair caught up in a roll at the nape of her neck. She wore only a trace of make-up and plain country clothes; her long hands were devoid of all jewellery except her gold wedding ring.

'Are you coming down?' she called again, taking out her coat from the hall cupboard and adjusting her hat in the spotted mirror. Vicky came skipping down the stairs in her stockinged feet, full of excitment. She danced around Liz, impatiently hopping from one foot to the other while waiting for her Wellingtons to be fitted. As Liz pushed on Vicky's boots, Evelyn appeared on the stairs.

They went out of the gate at the bottom of the garden, Evelyn carefully shutting it behind them while Liz strode on ahead up the usual path beside a grassy field. At the top of the hill she stopped and looked across the countryside, taking in deep breaths of air. Behind her she heard Evelyn and Vicky stopping to look at an indignant hedgehog; and then the story of Mrs Tiggywinkle retold in Evelyn's patient tones.

As she stood high above the neighbouring fields, she saw a group of schoolboys earnestly playing cricket some distance away. While she watched, a slim young boy in slightly muddied whites ran up to the crease and leapt forwards high into the air, his right arm curving upwards in a perfectly coordinated throw – the ball flew towards the far wicket. Liz's eyes followed him. Just like Jack, she thought; he was beautiful. She had often stood in the sun by the pavilion watching her brother Jack play. A natural leader, he had captained the school cricket team. She had always been so proud to be his sister, squirming with delight at every success.

Everyone admired Jack. He was the intelligent one who had always achieved high marks effortlessly at school. He was the great success of the family while she had struggled along, always just that little bit behind. Now she missed him – missed his friendship, his enthusiasm, the aura of excitement that surrounded him.

Liz stood there for a long time, half seeing the sandy-haired bowler and half seeing Jack. She had forgotten her mother and her five-year-old daughter Vicky. Her hand resting on an elm tree, her heart was back in the days when she and Jack had been at boarding-school, the girls' section separated from the boys' except on those glorious days when the girls were allowed to be spectators at cricket matches. She could still taste the sweetened orange juice and the little dry cakes they had inevitably had for tea.

During the treasured holidays nothing had separated them, and she remembered lovingly rubbing linseed oil into his bat before every match. They had been a good team.

Evelyn came up behind her.

'It's starting to rain, I think it would be better for Vicky if we went in,' she said.

Vicky's wearing her Wellingtons, thought Liz, and anyway it isn't coming down very hard. She wished her mother would stop interfering with the child. Evelyn had seemed to be trying to take over ever since they had come down to Devon to stay with her.

She heard Vicky's shrill little voice calling. 'Look, Mummy! Look, Granny!'

They looked. Liz's daughter was walking along the low crumbling wall beside the path, her arms stretched out either side of her for balance. Under her mackintosh she wore home-made dungarees and a cherry-red thick-knit jumper – and of course the Wellington boots. Her arms wavered slightly, but she regained her balance quickly, stopping only momentarily.

'Aren't you clever, darling!' Liz called over to her.

Evelyn hurried back down the path to where Vicky was playing and Liz followed her mother slowly. They watched her progress along the wall until she reached a gate.

'Careful! Don't forget to bend your knees when you jump down,' warned Evelyn. Vicky jumped happily and Liz caught her and swung her round to the ground. She scampered on ahead of them up the path.

'Vicky's just like Jack, quite fearless – not like you, you were always far more cautious,' Evelyn remarked.

Liz sighed, resenting her mother's long-held assumptions about the difference between her and Jack. Jack had been Evelyn's favourite and she had always expected him to be more daring and exciting than Liz. Not that Evelyn had seen that much of her children when they were growing up but now, nearly sixty and a widow, she was obviously pleased that the war was giving her a chance to get to know her daughter and granddaughter better. Perhaps, Liz thought, if her mother had spent more time with both of them she would have noticed Liz more. It was a bit late now.

Evelyn broke into her thoughts.

'But look where it got him,' she continued bitterly. 'It still hasn't sunk in, you know. I keep expecting him to stroll up the drive in his RAF uniform.'

Liz still found it too painful to talk to her mother about Jack; it was impossible to imagine his body lying dead somewhere. She could not believe that the brother she had been so close to – needed so much – was dead.

All her resentment and anger about the waste of Jack's life had to be held back. She had always been so cool and assured, so careful; she had played safe with her marriage to Laurence – the 'right' class of man – and their well-planned daughter. Now she felt blown off-course by a deep grief over her brother's death and a frustrated urge to do something. With the war and the horror of losing Jack, Liz felt that all her insecurities had been exposed.

As Liz walked on down the glistening Devonshire lane, raindrops fell on the hedgerows which were spotted with little mauve and blue flowers. Vicky had found a tree to swing from and now she swung and grinned, showing off her dimples, happy and muddy. Evelyn stood watching her, tidy as ever in her tweed coat and skirt. The war seemed so far away. This was a moment she would like to have shared with Jack, but the war had erased that possibility. She loathed it with an intensity of which she would never have believed herself capable.

Evelyn's thoughts had been following the same lines and now she turned to Liz.

'If we'd been able to bury him here, with your father . . . ' she began.

Liz could barely bring herself to respond, but she felt the same.

'I hate to think of him rotting out there,' she agreed.

It was unbearable that no one really knew what had happened to Jack's body. Blown up with the plane he was piloting, had been the official conclusion.

That afternoon Liz sat sewing diligently with other local women. Quite a number from the village had joined Evelyn's weekly 'Make Do and Mend' sessions, though at first there had been rumblings in the village about 'that woman in the big house telling us what to do'.

The women, a few with children, were sitting in the cluttered front room. They were no longer distracted by the spectacle of the exotic fripperies collected by Evelyn during her years aboard: the chain of ivory elephants, the south Indian silk weavings and the Rajasthani wood carvings. Instead they concentrated on their sewing and knitting, unravelling wool from old jumpers. One young woman was painstakingly cutting out usable cloth from old garments and folding the pieces neatly beside her.

As they worked, the women discussed their latest news. They began gossiping about recent events in the village, such as the goings-on of some of the young wives whose husbands were away in the Forces. Naturally enough, they progressed to talking about the news from their own absent sons and husbands. Most seemed to know where their men were serving, although open references had been censored from their letters. They compared notes on the relative comforts and dangers of the various postings.

Mrs Simpkins from the baker's shop interrupted, commenting, 'Careless talk costs lives' and putting a finger to her lips; but the flow of talk washed over her admonitions. After all, most of the women in the room had known each other all their lives.

Carefully Liz pulled her needle through the thin cotton fabric, blocking out the constant chatter and concentrating as she pushed it in again. She pricked her finger and put it to her mouth to suck away the blood, wishing yet again that they had managed to get enough thimbles to go round. She had lent hers to Mrs Pritchard from the village, who sat in a deep armchair across the room clumsily tacking together pieces cut from an old winter coat to make a siren suit for her toddler son.

Leaning across Vicky, who was wrestling with a large pair of drumstick knitting-needles, Liz turned up the knob on the wireless. She would rather hear the announcer than those voices droning away. As the others chatted and pondered hemlines, Liz listened with growing interest to an appeal from the BBC:

When every possible source of information about that area had been thoroughly combed for details, we still lacked an actual picture of those few hundred yards of France to complete our knowledge, and it is in this connection that you can see how this talk affects you personally.

Liz leaned closer to the set and held her needle poised while Vicky squirmed annoyingly in her seat. The broadcast continued:

Quite by chance it transpired that one of the staff officers working on the plan had spent a holiday in the Bruneval neighbourhood just before the war . . .

'Mummy, I've dropped another stitch,' Vicky cut in and Liz turned to give her attention to her daughter.

'Oh dear, let's see,' she said brightly as she looked at the oddly-shaped, lumpy piece of red knitting and tried to work out how many stitches there had been in the first place. At the same time she kept one ear on the clear BBC voice:

. . . He looked through it and there, sure enough, were photographs taken on his holiday showing in minute detail the exact spot concerned.

Vicky pulled at her arm.

'Shh, darling, show it to Granny; Mummy's trying to listen,' Liz whispered urgently.

It was five of those photographs put together that formed the last link in the whole plan.

Evelyn was reassuring Mrs Pritchard about the siren suit when Vicky, clutching the bold red knitting, began trying to climb on her grandmother's lap.

'It is very smart, my dear,' soothed Evelyn. Vicky clamoured for attention, pinching Evelyn's arm.

'Granny, Granny, what about mine?'

So you see . . . private photographs helped to ensure the successful operation in Bruneval; snapshots taken in the carefree pre-war days without any thought of their later value. There are thousands of such photographs in this country. I ask you to lend those photographs to the Admiralty.

In her mind's eye Liz could see her own holidays in France, that wonderful gooey cheese and the walks in the countryside when staying with her friend Claudine. She could picture Claudine now, eating her morning croissant cautiously in order to prevent the outer layer flaking off and making a mess. Her own croissant, Liz remembered, had always been partially drowned in her bowl of strong black coffee before she wolfed it down. She laughed to herself . . . and then thought more seriously of her last holiday in France by the seaside with Laurence and Vicky. She knew she had put the photos in an album somewhere; it was just a question of finding the album.

Vicky came over and gave her a hug. 'Look, Mummy, Granny mended my knitting.'

Matty's mind wandered in agitation as her swift fingers continued with the monotonous process of picking out and joining together pieces of metal. Next to her, Joyce picked up the parts once again and stamped them with a little gadget which made a repetitive sizzling noise and a sour, unpleasant smell. Vera Lynn had been played all afternoon over the Tannoy, and some of the girls were still enjoying it. Matty had begun to feel impatient with the eternal whine.

In the small Wapping factory, two dozen women concentrated on making machine parts for the Royal Engineers. There were one or two older men and young boys amongst them, but to all intents and purposes the place was a female domain. They all knew what a vital link they were in the war effort – Churchill had come and told them in person.

Matty knew she looked rather attractive in her factory overalls, with her dark hair spilling out of her head-scarf, and she wished the effect weren't so wasted. She gazed at herself admiringly in the dull window. If only she didn't look so pale from the long hours spent indoors! She pinched her cheeks to improve her colour and Joyce looked up at her friend and winked.

'You doing anything tonight, Matty?'

'No, why?'

'Thought you were primping yourself up for the boys,'

she teased. 'Why don't we go up the Palais?'

'See if there are any Yanks about?' suggested Matty, and both girls laughed and raised their eyebrows.

Matty's face grew serious – for her it wasn't so simple. She knew she would have to think what to do about her mother first; she couldn't just go out on the town and leave her.

Quiet, gentle Aimée – she looked rather faded now, though she wasn't that old – was stuck at home. Her face told the story of all they had been through together when fleeing from Nazi-occupied France. The two of them had been left to escape on their own. Matty's father, Ron, had gone back to England earlier to join the Allied Forces in Italy – not anticipating any possibility of the Germans marching in and taking over their home town, and underestimating the danger his wife would be in because she was Jewish. Aimée and Matty had escaped by hiding in the back of a coal-truck beneath stifling sacks of coal, travelling through road blocks, driving by night down bumpy tracks and eventually managing to get aboard a ship to England.

Matty had used all her resources of ingenuity to get them to safety, had even done things she would never be able to tell Aimée. Now her mother remained with Ron's father, Albert, in his small shabby dwelling in the East End. Aimée was listless, homeless, husbandless and miserable. She had virtually given up on life, trapped in a deep inescapable gloom.

Joyce guessed what her friend was thinking and felt a sudden anger towards Aimée. Matty should have the chance to get out and enjoy herself and not have to stay in constantly to nanny a malingering mother.

'Still the same, is she?' she enquired.

'Yes,' Matty said shortly.

'About time she snapped out of it,' retorted Joyce unsympathetically.

'There's some things you don't snap out of . . . ' Matty said angrily, and Joyce's broad freckled face stared at her in surprise. Joyce had never had to escape from any danger; she had no real idea of the war as it was on the ground in France, Matty thought.

'You are my sunshine, my only sunshine . . . ' came blasting over the factory Tannoy. All these English thought they were so safe! Damn them for being so wrapped-up in their own lives. Matty looked round defiantly and, conducting wildly with both arms, led a rousing chorus of a crude version of the song.

As they left the factory at the end of their shift, Matty told Joyce that she had thought of a way to get out of her responsibility for the evening. If she could get hold of a packet of cigarettes, she would be able to bribe her grandfather to look after Aimée for her, and then they could go to the dance at the Palais.

The girls stopped off at the local amusement arcade since Matty's best chance to win some cigarettes was at the shooting range. She paid for a round and, with the rifle firmly in her hands, managed to shoot her way to the prize of a packet of Woodbines. Triumphantly she and Joyce went home to get ready to go out.

Matty hung around by the doorstep of the two-up, two-down terraced house, waiting for her grandfather to appear. She knew he would come out right on the hour; he worked his allotment as regular as clock-work.

Albert opened the door and Matty managed a casual, 'Hello, Grandad. Off to the allotment?'

He was not taken in by her for a moment – he knew her too well by now not to recognize when she was after something, and his opinion was confirmed when she pulled out the packet of Woodbines.

'What are you after then?' he asked suspiciously.

'Mum all right?' asked Matty in return, nodding towards the house.

'Dancing on the ceiling,' Albert responded sourly. Then he looked down at the packet of Woodbines clutched in her hand and relented.

'All right,' he said. 'I know. I'll stay with your mum tonight. Bloody nursemaid, that's what I am!'

Matty handed over the cigarettes. 'Thanks. See you in an hour or so.'

She kissed the small, wiry Cockney she loved on his rough cheek and almost danced over the threshold and into the house. Albert shook his head and plodded off down the road, dragging a large garden fork he had brought from the kitchen.

'Hello, Mum. I'm home!' Matty called loudly as she banged the door behind her. Aimée, looking pale and haggard, was sitting at the kitchen table which was covered with a red gingham cloth. She barely noticed Matty's cheery entrance as she continued stitching a Union Jack; a small pile of finished ones lay beside her. Lost in a confusion of misery, she hardly seemed to notice anything around her. Matty went over and gave her a big kiss but as usual there was no reaction.

'I'll make a nice cuppa,' Matty said, clattering about the kitchen.

But Aimée was barely aware of her presence as she filled the kettle, placing it on a gas ring and hunting for the matches on an untidy shelf containing old pots and pans and a much used brown oven-dish. As Matty lit the gas and found a teapot and two biscuits, she chattered brightly about the events of her day, but there were tears at the back of her eyes.

*

19

Later that evening Joyce and Matty were having a really good time at the Palais. Under the bright lights colourful couples twirled on the parquet floor while the band – smart in their black dinner-jackets – played a medley of popular tunes. At the edge of the dance floor little tables overflowed with laughing groups on their night out. Matty was dancing herself off her feet, wearing a glamorous outfit of her own concoction made from net curtains and black-out material sewn together in a daring combination. She had even managed to paint her lips a deep scarlet, though what the 'lipstick' had started out as she preferred not to say. A curly-haired soldier came up to her as she rested momentarily by the bar and looked at her appreciatively.

'You dancing?'

'You asking?' retorted Matty.

'I'm asking.'

'Then I'm dancing!' They both laughed and he put his arm round her waist as he escorted her to the floor. Then, emboldened by his success, he tried another line.

'Anyone ever told you you look like Vivien Leigh?'

Matty, as always, had a quick reply to hand.

'Yes. Must've been the same line-shooter who said you looked like Clark Gable!'

He grinned. 'I can see you're my type.'

They both noticed a sign by the dance floor which read 'No jitterbugging'.

'Scared you'll be court-martialled?' Matty dared him. He swung her around and they jived, madly and joy-fully.

The music changed after that to *J'attendrai*.

'How is your foxtrot?' Matty asked breathlessly.

'Not Jatton-bloody-Dray!' said the soldier, trying to draw Matty off the dance floor. 'That's what they ought to ban. Won't catch me dancing to no frog music. Dirty traitors!'

Matty was furious.

'What do you know about it?' she asked indignantly, determined not to let him get away with such prejudice.

'I know I wouldn't let the Jerries walk into *my* country!' he retorted. Matty had a clear vision of the streets packed with refugees loaded down with all their possessions – behind them the German troops advancing mercilessly.

'We'd give them a fight if they landed here, not just surrender,' he continued. 'Even de Gaulle scarpered.'

Matty interrupted his flow: 'Only so as he could fight back from here!'

But he ignored her and went on, ' . . . And look at 'em now, licking the Nazis' boots. Filthy collaborators!'

Matty could not take any more, so she raised her hand and slapped him hard across the face. There was a startled silence and then a crowd began to gather around them, including some of the girls from the factory, several men in Navy uniform and an RAF sergeant.

'Bloody hell!' exclaimed the soldier, rubbing his cheek.

As Joyce tried to restrain Matty, she launched forth into a tirade.

'You don't know a sodding thing about it! Not about the ordinary French people. What choice did they have? And what do you think it's like for them now? Back in the autumn, fifty people were shot down in cold blood in Bordeaux because someone killed a German officer. Did you know that? No, you didn't, did you? So just you shut your bloody mouth!' She stormed off across the dance floor.

A few minutes later she was standing beside the bar,

still seething. None of the English seemed to understand what the French were going through. Just see how they would feel if their mothers ended up like hers!

A tall RAF sergeant tapped her on the soldier. 'Your friend just told me you're half French?' he queried.

'Yes, and not ashamed of it either,' she answered fiercely.

'All right, keep your hair on!' he placated her. 'Do you speak French fluently?'

'Like a bleeding native.'

'They're looking for people who do. You could use the lingo to help your pals over there.'

Matty was intrigued; *this* was something she could do. She took down the phone number he offered.

In Vicky's bedroom with its light blue walls and dormer windows covered with blue-flowered curtains, Liz was reading her a bed-time story. She sat on the edge of the bed, making a dent in the regular pattern of the patchwork quilt. A small reading light was on and Vicky cuddled up to her much loved teddy bear, Blue Ted – though he wasn't quite the same brilliant blue as when Jack put him down beside her only hours after she had been born.

'So Kanga and Roo stayed in the forest,' read Liz, 'and every Tuesday Roo spent the day with his great friend Rabbit, and every Tuesday Kanga spent the day with her great friend Pooh, teaching him to jump, and every Tuesday Piglet spent the day with his great friend Christoper Robin. So they were all happy again.'

Liz bent and kissed the soft rose-petal cheek of her daughter.

'One for me and one for Daddy,' she said, kissing her twice.

'When are Daddy and Uncle Jack coming home?' asked Vicky and Liz thought again of her brother as she had last seen him in his smart RAF uniform, standing brave and dear, going on enthusiastically about how he was going to stop the war. She considered what to tell a five-year-old.

'Darling, Uncle Jack isn't going to come back.' She knew that the difference between Uncle Jack's eternal absence and Daddy's temporary posting overseas was incomprehensible to her daughter and hoped that death would continue to be a distant mystery to Vicky for many years yet.

Later that evening Liz sat quietly at her glass-topped dressing-table, surrounded by photos of Laurence, Jack and Vicky, and of her parents when younger. Spread out at one side of the dressing-table was her set of silver-backed initialled hairbrushes and a collection of silver-topped bottles. Picking up an album from a pile at her feet, she flipped through the pages looking for pictures of France. Most recently these had been of holidays on the north-west coast with Laurence and Vicky, but she looked eagerly for earlier pictures of time spent as a schoolgirl and student with her best friend Claudine. She remembered so many different times, parties and events – seeing herself as she was on her initial visit to Paris. Her first encounter with Claudine was vivid in her mind and she recalled the incredible sophistication and glamour of the young girl with dark hair drawn into the chic style of a woman.

At that moment Evelyn walked in and she looked suspiciously at the French albums. Liz explained she had been thinking about Claudine and wondering what might have happened to her.

'I'm sure she's all right,' said Evelyn. 'That girl knows how to look after herself.'

'How can you be all right in an occupied country?' answered Liz. 'I think of her, and I think of myself safe in boring Devon! I can't stand it . . . '

Evelyn remained silent; she seemed hurt. Contritely, Liz threw her arms around her mother. 'Can't you see that I want to do my bit, too?'

Colin was apprehensive when he was called from the mess to a meeting with the Lieutenant-Commander. As he walked through the Navy compound, he wondered which of his slip-ups had been discovered and mentally prepared himself as if this were another audition. Chin up, he thought, and endeavoured to look his most forceful and trustworthy as he went into the mustard-coloured office.

Lieutenant-Commander Arden looked up with real irritation; he had no patience with other units trying to steal his men. He regarded Colin dispassionately – a handsome, athletic lad with a face unmarked by experience, smartly turned out in his naval officer's uniform.

From the senior officer's hesitation, Colin saw that he was not in for the standard reprimand.

'An order has come through for you to report to a special unit in London,' Arden said. 'Don't ask me what it's about, I don't know. But I'm damned sorry to lose my French translator.'

Colin took his transfer orders, thinking how odd it was that his holidays in France had given him the one skill which had made him stand out in the Navy. Walking back to the barracks to pack his kit, he silently thanked his mother for her forethought in spending so much money on him and their holidays in France, and for indulging his passion for sailing. He had spent many happy hours speaking French with fellow yachtsmen who had become his friends.

Automatically folding his gear ready for the kit-bag, he wondered what rank he would have reached by this time had he not left after Naval College to go on the stage. How ironic, he thought, that the war should have thrown him back five years. Sometimes he wondered whether he was a serving officer or simply an actor who was playing the part. Any minute now the scene would end and he would find himself free on the road again. Dreams! He had his orders and he had to go. But he would make damn sure that before he left he got down to the bar to say goodbye to Jimmy and Simon and the others with whom he had shared the last two months.

Liz arrived at the West London address which had been detailed in her telegram, carrying her photograph album under one arm. She was wearing a discreet navy and white dress with a small hat and gloves to match, which she had carefully chosen for the occasion. Somehow the neat dress helped to hide her nerves as the War Office porter in his blue serge jacket with gold crowns on the shoulder escorted her through the imposing corridors of the requisitioned hotel. As he turned, she noticed with a sudden qualm that one sleeve was empty – a reminder of the reality of war.

She was shown into a starkly functional room which still bore traces of being a hotel bedroom; a headboard on one wall, a dusty wash-basin and elaborate fitted cupboards. The windows were boarded up and the only furniture remaining was a plain table and two office chairs. A single light-bulb hung in the centre of the room.

Behind the table sat a well-groomed auburn-haired woman of about forty who stood up and greeted Liz kindly.

'Come in, Mrs Grainger. I'm Faith Ashley.'

Liz hesitated. She had expected a man, an Army officer, and was taken aback to see a woman.

They shook hands and Faith took the photo albums, but Liz realized that she was less interested in them than in the answers to the questions that she fired at Liz.

'You're living in Devon?' Faith began.

'Yes,' Liz answered. 'I took my daughter down there when the Blitz started. We're living with my mother.'

'You have just the one child?'

'Yes.'

'How old is she?'

'Five.'

The questions about every aspect of her home life continued: about her husband, her mother, her own education and her brother Jack.

'He was shot down over Germany three months ago,' Liz said woodenly.

'I'm sorry. You were close?' asked Faith.

'Very. Our parents were stationed abroad during most of our childhood and we were rather thrown together.'

The questioning then turned to Claudine and these holidays in Bragues, in Normandy. She had to describe Claudine's family and also where her home was. Then without warning Faith began to speak in French; smoothly Liz switched over too.

'You certainly speak the language well,' Faith complimented her. 'Your knowledge of France and the French might be of use to the war effort.'

'You mean translating or something?' Liz answered. 'I'm afraid I could only do a part-time job because of my daughter Vicky. But if there is some part-time work, I'd very much like to be considered.'

Matty's interview started off on the wrong foot. Before she even got into the interview room, she laddered her stockings in the waiting-room and swore loudly at the damage.

'Bleeding heck!'

'Can I help? I've got some nail varnish.'

A quietly dressed girl who was coming out of the lift laughingly offered help and Matty put her leg up on a chair and applied the varnish to the end of the ladder. It was quickly done, but Matty's outburst had already been noted by her escort and it affected her record adversely.

She did not take to Faith, whom she considered hoity-toity and disapproving. Faith seemed surprised by the combination of Matty's East End English accent with Picardy-accented French, so Matty explained her background.

'You were in Picardy when the war broke out?' asked Faith.

'Yes, at my grandmother's guest-house,' Matty answered.

'Why didn't you and your family return to England?'

'Dad did,' Matty said proudly. 'He joined up in the British Army straight away, but Mum wanted to stay on. Grandma was getting too weak to move, so we kept on running the guest-house even though there were no guests. Before Grandma died, she made me promise to take Mum back to England.' She hesitated.

'So you did?' prompted Faith.

'Yes,' Matty answered, giving nothing away. She did not want to talk about her ordeal coming out of France. She felt Faith was unsympathetic and making snobbish judgements about her. Christ, she was proud of her East End origins; she wasn't going to cover them up.

Next, Faith started on another tack, asking about Matty's work experience.

'You name it! Waitress, hairdresser, shop assistant. I even did a stint in the post office as a wireless operator,' answered Matty defiantly. 'And now I'm a turner for my sins, making machine parts for the Royal Engineers.'

'And how do you enjoy that?' enquired Faith.

'I'm bored to buggery!'

Coming out of the War Office hotel, Liz saw the tempting sign of a café. She felt the need of refreshment after the surprising interview and decided to go in and have a pot of tea. Thoughts swam through her mind as she sat at the little table pouring milk into the blue china cup. It had not occurred to her that they might offer her a job and she wondered what Laurence's reaction would be. She considered how she might arrange to spend part of the week at their Knightsbridge flat and leave Vicky with Evelyn.

She was just pouring her second cup when a bouncing figure broke the peace. Matty, dying for a cup of tea too, had rushed into the same café.

'Yoo-hoo!' she called, waving as she spotted Liz. 'Remember me? Thanks again for the loan of the nail varnish,' she said breezily, sitting down at the table and ordering tea and 'cakes if there are any'.

'I'm Matty Firman,' she began. 'Who are you?'

'Liz Grainger.'

They discussed what the purpose of the interviews could have been. Matty was unimpressed by Faith, and thought she had ruined her own chances of getting a job anyway. Liz had never met anyone as brash as the dark-haired, vivacious, full-figured Matty. Happy to talk about herself, Matty described everything from the factory's monotony to Faith's snooty response to her swearing. Liz was amused by this prolonged outburst, but was not the sort of person to respond in kind. She could see that Matty was fun, though she was nervous of trusting her. Liz had been sobered by the implication that she had something to offer to the War Office and when Matty pressed her for information, she avoided giving the details of her interview; somehow she felt it would be the wrong thing to do.

Liz remained in London, having been warned of the possibility of a further interview. She had prepared herself for a job offer by the time she was called back to the War Office hotel two days later. This time she was interviewed by Colonal James Cadogan and was very impressed by this tall, elegant, balding officer with his piercing blue eyes and air of suppressed enthusiasm. He was particularly interested in her friend Claudine, wanting to know whether she still lived near Bragues. Liz did not really know, having had no contact with anyone in France since the Occupation. Colonel Cadogan, who appeared to be known affectionately as Cad, asked her clever leading questions which were obviously intended to determine her war-time allegiances.

'Are you seeking vengeance for your brother's death?' he asked. This was putting it too strongly for Liz.

'No,' she said hesitantly. It unnerved her that they must have run a check on both Laurence and Jack. How much more did they have on file about her, she wondered.

'Would you be prepared to return to France?' Cad

enquired. This was a totally unexpected request, for Liz had never considered that they would want her to do anything other than work in an office in London.

'You mean to the Unoccupied Zone?' she said.

'No,' replied Cad.

It was only then that Liz received a more detailed explanation of all this interest in her. Apparently they were sending agents into France, civilian as well as servicemen, to undermine the enemy. The greater shock for Liz was that they were sending in women as well as men to do this dangerous work. Cad was clear and convincing about her importance to their operation.

'You speak fluent French. You know the country well. Such specialized knowledge is invaluable to our cause and very hard to come by. You needn't give me an answer now. Think it over and let me know when you've decided.'

Vicky was uppermost in her mind and there was nothing to decide. She had not appreciated the extent of what they might ask her to do.

'I'm sorry, Colonel,' she said, 'but I couldn't even consider it. I have a young child.'

It was very different for Matty at her second interview. Cad kept a sharp eye on her when he explained that he wanted her to return to France as a British agent. She did not resemble the subordinates he had commanded in his previous commission as a regular officer in the Army; she was not even his usual FANY material: educated girls from good homes. Nor was he immediately sure what to make of her. A stocky girl of medium height, sallow skin contrasting with dark hair – she looked like the factory girl she was. In English her voice was

Cockney and her vocabulary was working class. In French she had absorbed the milieu of her mother's relatives and sounded as if she came from a prosperous background. He thought wryly that what puzzled him would certainly puzzle the Germans, but she would be useful material as she had scored exceptionally highly in the intelligence test.

Her face lit up as she realized what she was being offered. 'I don't even need to consider it. Send me out there tomorrow if you like.'

Cad slowed her down because he wanted her to understand the full implications.

'First you'd be put through a rigorous training and we would have to assess your performance.'

Matty was not interested in long explanations. It was her own country the Germans were tramping over and she was ready to fight back now. More than that, she felt she had no choice but to fight the Germans – as a Jew, she would be first on their list if they got to Britain.

Cad reminded her that the job would involve leaving her mother, and she should think carefully about what effect that might have. Matty knew what he was referring to; the strain of their escape had pushed her mother to the borderline of sanity. She recalled the days buried in the back of a slowly labouring truck under dusty sacks of coal, mouths full of choking black dust. Every time the vehicle slowed down with a groan of brakes, their imaginations would envisage German soldiers opening the back of the truck: first pulling out some of the sacks, then finding the two of them and knowing they were Jewish. Discovery would have meant deportation to Germany. The Nazis had succeeded in breaking her mother and it would multiply their successes if Matty herself gave in. She thought of her father fighting in Italy

– he had wangled his way into the British Army despite his age. If anyone could stop the Nazis, thought Matty high-spiritedly, the Firman family would!

Cad, Faith, Gil Acworth – the group's planning officer – and Victor Travussini, the briefing officer, met in Cad's office for their weekly briefing session. Cad chain-smoked from behind his over-large desk which took up half the floor space of the office. Gil, a short man who looked as though he should be running a branch post office and who had an obsession with forms and details, coughed and crossed the room to open the window. Victor lounged elegantly on the sofa like a bored aristocrat, waiting to begin. His Italianate looks and smouldering manner amused Faith; she thought he looked more like a gigolo than a military officer.

They began with an overview of all the Areas they were working in; for each they had to consider the most appropriate network. In some, messages could be carried by couriers; in others, most communication passed through neutral embassies; the most problematic Areas relied totally on 'pianists' – radio-operators. Some networks could utilize existing Free French contacts and strong underground movements which had preceded the arrival of the British; others had to rely on doubtful Communist connections who might use donated weapons for their own ends.

Area 3, centered on the port town of Bragues, had become a major disaster as four agents had been lost to the Germans in a single month. What they needed was more information – and for that they needed more agents. The men turned to Faith for information on the latest trawl for recruits and she began by giving a brief summary of the eight possibles.

'I've sounded out six of them,' Cad confirmed. 'We're expecting their decisions any time now.'

Victor and Gil listened to the character references in silence. Victor's prejudices were aroused by the mention of Colin Beale's profession; he was worried about actors being 'pansies' and perhaps unreliable.

'What sort of chap would leave the Navy for a job like that?'

Cad responded by reminding him that some of their most successful agents had been second-hand-car merchants, archaeologists and even journalists! Gil was more worried that three of the civilian recruits were women. Both Cad and Faith were sure that the use of female agents in France was essential, but Gil had other views on women in this role.

'Yes,' said Faith drily, 'they're emotional, weak, intellectually inferior . . . '

'There's no getting away from it,' Gil responded. 'They're a liability. No offence, Faith; I don't count you as one.'

Faith assumed that this was supposed to be a compliment. Since the war started she had found solace for her broken marriage in the role of intelligence officer. It was true that she had never managed to successfully combine being a wife and a working woman, but Gil's assumption that her efficiency in the Outfit ruled out her femininity was thoughtlessly cruel. She would fight to make sure the women she recruited would have the best possible chance. Meanwhile, she did not think it worth replying to Gil's remark.

Colonel Heinz Krieger sat alert in his staff car as he was driven into the small town of Gouloncourt where he had been billeted. Although he looked the archetypal Nazi –

being tall, blue-eyed and greying-blond – he was not a Nazi ideologue, having joined the Party four years earlier solely to advance his career. As a patriot he knew how much the previous war had humiliated his country and was willing to stand up for Germany's rights. Once the war had begun, it was clear that he could not continue in his job as an interpreter and salesman for an export company, so he had joined Intelligence in order to remain in an office job. He was now forty-four years old and married with two sons – he had no wish to see active service at the front.

The only pleasing thing about his posting was that he had heard from the previous encumbent that he had requisitioned a rather splendid French château. Not only that, but the lady of the house was a divorced and extremely attractive woman, Claudine de Valois, who was apparently responsive to the charms of a German officer. She had moved into a small gatehouse that bordered the road, but it was still near enough – he had been assured – for easy access. Krieger smiled. There were some compensations for being posted to such a provincial spot.

Liz could not sleep. Getting out of bed, she pulled her sensibly quilted dressing-gown around her shoulders and went over to sit at her dressing-table. She made an attractive picture as she sat there – ruffled fair hair loose on her shoulders, white nightdress visible beneath an azure gown. She looked at herself in the mirror and then down at the framed photo of Jack, who smiled back at her.

If she decided to reconsider and go to France, Vicky would have to be sent away to school and Evelyn would have to take all the responsibility for her during the holidays – would this be fair to either of them? And what would Laurence think? He saw her as a wife and mother, but perhaps he would understand the importance of this particular use of her special skills. She had so much to offer; she had spent years in France, had studied at the Sorbonne and had reliable friends over there. This was the test. She looked at the life she was leading in Devon, becoming more like her mother every day. It was a new age; with the war on, all women were being called on to do their duty and were going out to do war work. Perhaps by taking the initiative she would be more like Jack, and in her own way carry on some small part of his fight.

Liz had made her decision: she was going to take the job.

Nevertheless, the thought of Vicky tugged at her heart and she stood up, opened her heavy bedroom door and crept out into the creaking passageway. In the darkness she felt the familiar way to the child's room. The door was open, but everything was black. Vicky's even breathing came clearly as Liz crossed the soft carpet to the window and pulled open the curtains so that the moonlight entered, gently illuminating the sleeping features. She looked down at her daughter. One day she would grow up – what sort of world would she have to face?

Matty knew she would find Albert working his allotment that evening and thought it a good place to talk to him. She slipped out of the house and knocked on the kitchen window next door. The continuous row of grey houses opened straight on to the pavement, and anyone passing could hear every word said inside them; there was no chance of keeping secrets from neighbours. Mrs Topolski's lined face appeared at the steamed-up window.

'Will you come and sit with my mum?' Matty asked. Mrs Topolski agreed and came out in her slippers and grease-splattered apron as Matty scooted off up the road.

As she came over the hill by the railway tracks she could see the dear, solid figure digging determinedly. She had decided to tell her grandfather before she rang Colonel Cadogan with her decision to accept.

Albert was not sympathetic to her desire to join the FANYs; he had seen her take too many jobs and throw them over too easily.

'They're a load of stuck-up toffee-nosed tarts, those fannies. Why d'you want to join them?' He did not wait for an answer. 'How much are they paying you, then?'

Matty had to confess that she had not enquired.

'Well,' he warned, don't you go chucking up that job at the factory until you've asked . . . ' She wondered if this was the moment to bring up the fact that she would be away most of the time.

Matty was impatient with the situation she was caught in. Her mother, who should have been a support, had collapsed; and it was her grandfather – with whom she had hardly spent any time – that she now had to look to. There was so much she had to offer and this was the first time she had had a chance to use her potential in something that would really grip her. She could not believe that her grandfather would let her down. Albert knew how much this meant to her and reluctantly agreed that she should take the job, but he could not resist a final grumble.

'Aimée's in a bad enough state without her only daughter gadding off . . . '

*

It was an overcast morning outside the elegant red-brick mansion block in which the Outfit was housed. Baker Street was dismal; there were not many people about and the shops were empty or boarded up as a result of the bombing.

A small figure could be seen emerging from the tube. In her FANY uniform Matty walked erect, proud of her status and determined to show her spunk. She wondered how many other girls she had seen wearing the FANY uniform were, like herself, working under cover for the Outfit. In front of the mansion block a taxi drew up with a clatter and Liz got out looking neat and immaculate, her hair tightly rolled below her cap. She paid off the driver and turned, to see Matty; they were both surprised and pleased at the sight of a familiar face.

'Why, you dark horse!' said Matty and they laughed. It was hard to believe that they were going to be secret agents.

A motor-cycle roared up Baker Street towards them. A figure in navy blue, his face concealed by goggles, zoomed past them, splashing them with dirty puddle water, and drew up at the pavement a few yards on. The driver took off his goggles and wolf-whistled. The girls glared back at him and flounced into the building while Colin looked appreciatively at their retreating bottoms. With a springy step he followed them up the stairs, making no effort to suppress his broad grin.

CHAPTER 2

Matty and Liz sat huddled together in the back of a large black car; they were being driven down through the countryside by a stiff-backed female officer. Both of them stared out of the window, watching the fields sweep by. Matty was eagerly enjoying the novelty of the green fields and the lazy cows, worlds away from Wapping and her boring factory job. She was able to relax rather more than Liz, living life for the moment. Matty had been through so much already in the war, that she had few worries about a training course.

They both found it remarkable that events had moved so quickly. They had arrived at Parkgrove Mansions in uniform for the first time, undergone a military briefing, been overwhelmed by quantities of instructions and solemnly warned of the rigours of the course. Now they were on their way to begin training for the mysterious Outfit, at Ettingley Manor.

'Hey, that must be it!' Matty whispered loudly to Liz. She could just make out the shape of a large manor house, some way in the distance and partially hidden amongst trees. Liz did not respond, which agitated her.

The car swung round a corner, the broad tyres scrunching on the gravel drive which was bordered by bushy rhododendrons and melancholy laburnum trees. The vast grey-stone house loomed before them, its castellated windows with grey leaded panes staring at them blankly. Matty thought it was just like the pictures and that Basil Rathbone ought to be striding out to greet them. She was getting more excited by the minute and she bounced in her seat, causing the springs to creak alarmingly and the officer driver to turn briefly and express her disapproval with a look.

'Flippin' heck. Look, Liz!' She hurried to correct herself. 'I mean Celeste.'

Matty blushed at her mistake, but the effect was lost on Liz whose thoughts were far away from their new surroundings. They were only supposed to know each other by their code names. Matty called herself 'Aimée' after her mother, while Liz, exerting a sense of humour, had chosen 'Celeste' after the female elephant in one of Vicky's favourite stories: *Babar the Elephant*. It was only because the girls had met earlier at their initial interviews that they had exchanged real names, and these they now attempted to keep to themselves.

Liz was thinking guiltily about leaving her daughter, already missing her she looked down at a small photograph of Vicky in a neat leather frame on her lap, a poor substitute for the real thing. Noticing the photo, Matty momentarily forgot her own excitement and looked at Liz with sympathy.

It was 1.15 a.m. – Liz had noted the time by the large institutional clock on the dormitory wall – when she was awakened roughly and dragged from her bed. Half-asleep, she stumbled down the corridor, forced through the dim light by the strong hands of two burly, uniformed soldiers. They manhandled her, not even giving her time to catch her breath before pushing her through a doorway and down a narrow staircase into a dingy grey cellar. A single, dazzlingly strong light glared at her from its position on a bare wooden table-top in the centre of the room. Liz blinked and staggered slightly as she was released. Her hands went up automatically to rub her upper arms where red marks stood out on the white flesh. The guards hovered at either side of her, ready to restrain any sudden movement.

Liz stood dazed in the bright light, child-like and painfully vulnerable in her regulation nightdress. She tried to see, but could not make out how many people were in the room around her. It was the moment all the recruits dreaded, the mock interrogation which could happen to any of them at any stage of their training, at any time of the day or night. The interrogation was carried out in harrowing earnest.

'What is your name?' a heavy German accent articulated from the far side of the table. With some difficulty Liz found herself able to focus on the man whom she now saw was seated at the table. He was well built and wore a German military uniform.

She looked straight into his eyes. 'Celeste Sarasin,' she replied.

'Where do you live?' the German continued.

'Number 7, Rue St Denis.' Liz had learnt her cover story so well that she almost believed it.

'Do you live on your own?'

'No, with Monsieur and Madame Ferrand. I look after their children.'

'How long have you been in their employment?'

'Six months.' The answers were coming more easily to her.

'Do you know a man called Cyprien?' he enquired, changing his tack.

Liz hesitated for a second; she had not expected this question.

40

'I don't think so . . . no.' She found herself taking rapid breaths, her heart beating loudly in her breast. She forced herself to be calm and breathe slowly and deeply.

The German noticed this and ventured unpleasantly, 'Perhaps you know him by another name. An English name?'

'I know no Englishman.'

'Are you sure, Mam'selle?'

'Yes.' She answered nervously and waited a moment for him to speak again.

'You are lying!' he shouted suddenly and more loudly than she had expected.

She flinched. 'No, I'm not, I . . . ' she trailed off.

'Then how is it that you were seen talking to him on Tuesday afternoon in the Café Balzac?' he continued harshly.

'I don't know what you mean.'

'Were you in the Café Balzac on Tuesday afternoon?'

'Yes, but . . . ' She wasn't given the chance to finish.

'Who was the man you spoke to?'

'I spoke to no one; I went in to kill time.'

Her interrogator looked at her coldly, then turned and nodded at the guard to her left. Liz felt the pain as her arm was twisted behind her and bit her lip but couldn't repress a small groan.

'It will be much easier if you tell me the truth. Did you speak to a man in the Café Balzac?'

'No. At least . . . ' She wasn't sure what she should say next. How much should she admit and how much should she go on denying? She hadn't yet had enough training for this. She panicked – what would happen if she got it wrong? She hesitated and then went on.

' . . . someone asked to look at my newspaper. Is that who you mean?'

'Who was he?' He spoke more patiently.

'I don't know. But he was French, not English.'

'Did you lend him your newspaper?'

'Yes.' She thought she should make this sound more reasonable. 'Well, I'd finished with it,' she continued.

'And he returned it to you?'

'Yes,' she replied.

'With a bundle of bank-notes tucked inside?' he queried.

'What?' Rather nervously, she tried to appear incredulous.

The impatient interrogator chose to ignore this and continued, 'Most of which were found on you when you were stopped yesterday?'

'No.'

Again he continued: 'No doubt on their way to finance some terrorist group.'

'That was my own money. I was on my way to the post office to pay it in – I told the officer,' she protested.

'Get over there!' the German shouted angrily. Liz was startled and confused: she looked round, but could not make out where he was pointing. Before she had a chance to move she found herself being grabbed from one side and shoved into the corner. The guard pushed her so hard that she stumbled and fell, dropping her right arm at an awkward angle in an attempt to break her fall. She winced. 'Get up!' The heavily-built German officer rose as he yelled at her and one of the guards pulled her roughly to her feet. She felt like a sawdust-filled doll with no initiative, no coordination.

'Put your hands on your head,' commanded the officer.

Liz could not move and the guard prodded her with his rifle, urging her to comply. She raised her arms clumsily and put her hands on her head, her right wrist throbbing.

'Now once again.' The interrogating officer walked

towards her from the table. 'Where did you get that money?'

Liz stood silently with her hands on her head, the pain in her wrist increasing every second. She watched the hands on the large clock on the wall behind the table move round . . . they seemed to move so very slowly. Gritting her teeth, she concentrated on the clock while her arms grew heavier and heavier.

The knowledge that this was only an exercise made it easier to bear. All she had to do was keep control and say only what she had learnt. The waiting couldn't go on for much longer, she thought; it was just a question of hanging on.

Two hours later Liz was still standing in the same position, her body aching with tiredness and strain. She began to worry about her cover story and thought of going over it again in her head, but she couldn't concentrate properly. She could only think of the relief she would feel if she could put her arms down, if she could rub her aching shoulders.

'I am still waiting.' The German voice broke into her thoughts.

'I didn't know the man. I'd never seen him before,' she whispered.

'Speak up.'

She coughed in an effort to clear her throat.

'The money was my own; I'd saved it from my earnings,' she continued, feeling he was not convinced. She must try to inject more honesty into her voice; she must sound real, otherwise she would not get through the interrogation. In France, her life would depend on getting it right.

'As a children's nurse?' He raised an eyebrow.

'Yes.'

'Monsieur Ferrand must pay you very well.'

'It was several months' salary. Plus a bonus from Madame – a birthday gift,' Liz explained hurriedly.

'And when is your birthday?' asked the German, hoping to catch her out. Liz paused for a moment, trying to think.

'June the seventh,' she said in some confusion, watching her interrogator look down quickly at his notes to check and then nod briefly as if reassured. She swayed slightly and reasoned that all she needed was to sit down for a moment, then she could gather her thoughts.

'Please may I sit down?' she ventured.

'No . . . ' One of the guards gave her a shove and it hurt.

' . . . When you tell me the truth, then you may sit down.'

Liz looked at him beseechingly. 'It is the truth,' she said but he ignored this statement.

'Where were you going with all that money?'

'To the post office.'

'You were going to the post office when you were stopped by my men?'

'Yes.'

'How long did you say you'd been living here, mam'selle?'

'Six months.'

'Then surely you must know that the post office is in the opposite direction,' he said, sounding pleased with himself.

Liz didn't have to put on any act to show the strain she was feeling by this stage. She felt sick and dizzy from standing with her hands on her head for so long, and also vulnerable standing there alone in her dark corner. She was tired from the days of early morning and evening runs, and the weapons and survival training. She was coping, but none of it had been easy. Now they had woken her in the middle of the night for this 'exercise' and she was no longer quite sure whether it was make-believe or true. She took a deep breath and thought: I must cope, I must do this right.

'I'm sorry . . .' she murmured. ' . . . I was confused.'

She watched the interrogator turn and say something in German to a guard standing to one side of the table. Then he turned back to her.

'Perhaps this will revive your memory!'

The guard hurled a bucket of cold water at her. It drenched her and she spluttered and shook her head about, wiping her hands over her face and hair. As she tried to shake off the water, the dampness crept down her body and her nightdress clung wetly to her bare skin. She felt close to real tears, horribly wet and miserable as she muttered her 'story within the cover story'. Now she had to fake a deep embarrassment.

'All right . . .' She paused. then hurried on. 'Most of what I said was true. I didn't know the man in the café, I promise I didn't. And the money was mine. Only . . . it wasn't my salary. Monsieur Ferrand gave it to me . . .' She trailed off, looking down shamefacedly and wishing she could make herself blush.

'He and I . . . You see . . . Madame Ferrand is an invalid and sometimes I . . .'

'Console him?' the interrogator finished for her.

'Yes.' Liz's voice was scarcely audible as she tried to feel the humiliation of revealing her 'indiscretion'.

'And what were you intending to do with the money?' he asked.

'I . . . I . . . ' Her mind seemed to have drifted away from the point.

'What?' he barked.

He spoke so abruptly that it made her start. Words would not come and she bit her lip. The pain generated a pulse of memory and she managed to regain some control, remembering to look down with shame once again.

'I was going to buy some new clothes on the black market.'

Liz didn't look up; she waited a moment, but nothing happened and in the lengthening pause she tried to sense their reactions – had she got it wrong? She couldn't see any of the soldiers properly and she didn't dare glance up.

The intense silence was broken at last.

'Now you may sit down.'

Liz sank down on to the bottom step of the wooden staircase – held together by fatigue, her legs askew, her nightdress clinging to her bare thighs, her hair wet and matted and clogged round her neck. She hardly noticed or cared as she heard the German voice of the interrogator change to a more kindly tone – the normal voice of Schweder, one of her instructors.

'That's enough for one night. Well done, Celeste! I think you deserve a brandy.'

With her head in her hands she choked back a sob, determined not to let them see her feelings.

Liz shut the dormitory door quietly behind her and crept towards her bed. It was nearly four o'clock in the morning and she didn't wish to wake the others. She saw Matty's bedside light go on, but not wanting to talk to anyone she rushed straight to the bathroom. However, Matty's piercing whisper reached her before she could close the door.

'How did it go?'

Liz wanted to whisper something back, but her whole body was trembling with nausea. She slipped into the bathroom and collapsed back against the door, closing it. Then she struggled across to the basin and stood for a second gripping the cold ceramic edge. Unable to retch she released her grip and sank down on the edge of the bath where she sat hunched, trying to control her shakes.

Matty lay in bed with her light on, not knowing whether or not to go after Liz. She decided to wait a little while, hoping that Liz would come out but, impatient to help and anxious, she only managed to wait five minutes before pulling back the blankets and getting out of bed. As she fumbled for her slippers she trod on something unfamiliar and heard a small crack. Alarmed, she crouched down and felt around for the object; picking it up, she saw that it was a small framed photo of a little girl – this must be Liz's daughter. The face in the photograph seemed very young and vulnerable. Matty took the photo over to Liz's bed and put it back under her pillow gently. Then she patted the pillow and went across to the bathroom.

In the gloom of the L-shaped room, Matty could dimly see the other two beds on either side of her. To the right lay Suzanne snoring mildly; the iron bedstead creaked as she rolled over. On her left Thérèse was tightly curled into a ball, her blankets almost on the floor. As Matty reached the bathroom door she looked back and the blackout curtains at the long windows stirred in a faint breeze. The room settled back into a rythmic quiet as the two sleeping women breathed together.

Matty pushed open the door and stood in the bath-room doorway, unable to see much and not liking to switch on the light. Gradually her eyes adjusted to the deeper darkness and she went over and perched on the bath beside the shivering Liz, putting an arm round her shoulder.

Liz was going over and over in her mind what had happened in the interview, worrying about her perfor-mance and dreading that she had not got the strength for the job. Again Matty asked her how things had gone.

'I don't know,' Liz answered miserably. 'I kept up the cover story, but . . . ' She did not want to admit how threatened she had felt, how they had worn away at her resolve. This was the first time that her normal emo-tional control had been made vulnerable.

Matty knew how alienating it felt to pass through danger and wanted to reassure Liz that she *had* suc-ceeded because her crucial last resolve had not snapped.

'Well done,' she said softly, trying to convey her sym-pathy. Liz reached over and held her hand, feeling Matty return her grip. She felt warmed by Matty's con-cern . . . able to think. The interrogation had ripped into her and stripped away her outer self. She could not remedy the sense of exposure, could not stop the feeling of violation and make herself whole again. The change engendered by this experience would remain with her for ever.

Matty felt Liz begin to straighten her back – the worst was over and they had shared their strength. Now Matty had seen Liz's reserves of courage while Liz had realized that underneath all her bravado Matty was capable of showing immense understanding and sympathy.

*

The recruits assembled as usual outside the main entrance of the manor house for the 7 a.m. run. They stood around in groups, leaning against the stone walls and chatting.

Matty had sunk down on the broad stone steps and saw through a haze of tiredness that one man in particular was exercising enthusiastically. Irritated by his violent movements and obvious cheerfulness, she just wanted to crawl back into bed. She had hardly slept last night, and knew that if she could not go back to bed she must ignore her tiredness, get up and prepare herself for the run. Just as she was staggering to her feet the over-enthusiastic recruit was rhythmically touching his toes; she noticed he was nicely proportioned, broad-shouldered with a straight back, strong legs and a firm bottom.

Matty was not going to let herself down; she would go on the run and do as well as anybody else. She joined the enthusiast saying, 'Let's warm up together.'

Colin, code name Cyrano, smiled easily in reply and began to jog on the spot and stretch out his arms. Matty also stretched out her arms and took deep breaths of cold country air. If she *must* punish her tired limbs, at least she could do it with a man she fancied!

Major Duncan, the Course Commandant – a wiry Scot in his late fifties – came briskly out of the front door.

'Right. Fall in!' he ordered. As they started to line up, Liz came running out.

'Just in time,' called Colin. Matty looked at her and thought she looked pale and out of breath already.

'Thought you'd been excused after last night,' Matty said as she joined them.

'I decided to come after all,' Liz answered resolutely.

'There's dedication!' teased Colin.

'Lunacy, you mean,' retorted Matty. 'I tell you one thing; when I get to France I shan't be doing any running before breakfast.'

'*If.*' Colin turned round to look at her quickly from his place ahead, just as the line started to head off down the gravel driveway. She had to wait a moment to catch her breath as they all began to run.

'What?' called Matty to the back of Colin's head.

'Don't forget we're only on trial,' he yelled as he strode athletically out of the gate and up the lane, leaving Matty and Liz trailing behind.

Half an hour later Liz was completely exhausted but she battled on regardless, concentrating only on putting one foot in front of the other along the narrow muddy lane. By this time she and Matty were right at the back of the line of runners. Ahead of them wiggled a snake of bobbing heads set on panting bodies harmonious in their identical kit – white Aertex shirts and brief blue shorts. Looking over her shoulder, Matty could see that Liz was not going to last much longer and slowed down deliberately to keep pace with her. At the rise of a small hill she stopped and bent over, panting and holding her side.

'Sod this for a lark!' she said to Liz, who had also stopped and was taking deep breaths to recover herself. The sweat glistened on her forehead and darkened the fair hair at her temples.

'Phew!' she exclaimed.

'You shouldn't have come – not after last night,' Matty reprimanded her.

'Matty . . . about last night. Thanks.'

'Forget it,' said Matty in a matter-of-fact way.

But Liz wanted to talk, to purge herself of the embarrassment caused by her loss of control the night before.

'I'm not one of the world's natural heroines,' she confessed, remembering the mock interrogation and how she had had to struggle to get through it.

'Who is?' replied Matty placatingly.

Liz thought how like Jack Matty was; she seemed to have his nerve, the courage to dive into things without even considering the dangers. Liz liked her for it and tried to explain what she meant.

'When I was being interrogated, I doubted whether I could cope in a real situation. Now I'm still trying to decide whether I'm up to it – not like you.'

Matty surprised her by answering, 'I reckon it's braver to think first, like you, and still go through with it.'

Liz looked doubtful, then the noise of footsteps on the stony lane broke the silence and the girls looked up to see Colin coming towards them.

'Don't tell me our star athlete's fallen by the wayside,' called Matty with feigned horror.

Colin had stopped ahead of them in the lane and was looking at something.

'Hey, Cyrano!' Matty called again, but Colin put his finger to his lips and hissed 'Ssh!' The girls joined him and he pointed to a clearing in the woods below where in the dappled shade of the trees they could see three young grey rabbits frolicking in the long grass. They had beautiful fluffy bodies and long pointed pinkish-grey ears, and they chased each other round in gleeful circles. Colin, Matty and Liz stood for a while in silence, just looking. This was the innocent England they were trying to preserve: they were being trained to kill for it.

It was Colin who eventually broke the mood. 'Better catch up with the others,' he said.

'You're kidding.' Matty couldn't for the life of her see that there was any hope.

'I was thinking of the short cut,' retorted Colin.

They followed him down a well-veiled turning off the lane and plunged into the woods. As they made their way through the damp undergrowth with brambles catching at their limbs, Matty swore inelegantly when her hair snagged on a trailing branch. Colin pulled them behind a thicket as they got to the bottom of the hill and they waited, grinning conspiratorially while the other runners came into view on the track beneath them. When the last one had passed, Colin nodded to Liz and Matty and they all crept out and into view on the track, joining in behind the column of runners as though they had been there all along. Colin, in splendid shape after his breather, accelerated and caught up with Pierre, a young Frenchman recently recruited to go back to France.

'Feeling the pace, old chap?' he called as he swept by easily with a leisurely stride. Pierre scowled at him and ran doggedly on at a slow, even pace. Major Duncan turned briefly and noted the two truants, but didn't seem to mind. Perhaps, Matty thought, he admired their initiative.

Training at Ettingley Manor continued for several weeks while they were taught techniques that might keep them alive in enemy territory. They were drilled on how to survive in the wild and their muscles were hardened by long forced marches, carrying heavy loads. They also worked with a comprehensive selection of explosives, learning how to set fuses and lay charges efficiently.

Matty went at everything physical with vigour, even the compulsory games, and constantly compared her progress with the others. Suzanne – a busty upper-class girl who always looked as if she had just come off the hockey-field, seemed to her to be the only other girl who was keen on sports. Matty found that in her own terms she was often competing with and therefore perhaps resenting Suzanne. She also discovered that she shone at shooting practice, though she concealed the fact that she had acquired her skill in an amusement arcade. She was pleased to note Danby and Major Duncan watching with approval when she started the shooting test. With exhilaration she raced successfully down the zig-zag path, through colourful rhododendron bushes coated in raindrops, using a Sten-gun to blast down pop-up targets. Not one remained standing.

The girls, who needed extra training, practised close combat on the lawn behind the manor house. So far as Matty was concerned, the only way to go about this was with as much ferocity as possible. She battled with her instructor, Danby, like a cornered alley-cat biting and scratching its way to freedom. He did his best to show her the recommended moves, calling out instructions as they fought, but Matty simply fought on using every dirty trick in the book and swearing profusely as she did so.

'Use the side of your hand, not your fist.' Danby's voice echoed round the terrace. 'Break the bugger's neck, not your knuckles!'

The men sat watching the women appreciatively and Colin joined Pierre, who looked a bit left out of the discussion on the last Australian cricket tour to Britain before the outbreak of war. Names such as Bradman, Fleetwood-Smith, Leyland and Hutton were bandied about, with scornful comments on the Australians' lack of bowlers at the final Oval Test.

Colin tried to get Pierre to talk about France, but the conversation lapsed because he was not allowed to reveal personal details, so Colin fell back on their shared enthusiasm for sailing.

As they talked, they continued observing the activity

on the lawn and admitted Matty's was a very successful method.

'The Queensberry rules don't get you far with the Nazis,' Colin remarked to Pierre from their vantage point. Secretly, he was impressed with Matty's performance.

Liz was more nervous than most about premeditated violence, but knew she must throw herself whole-heartedly into the training. In a clearing in the woods she crept up gingerly behind a lone figure in German uniform, brandishing what looked like a kitchen knife. Quickly she put her hand over his nose and mouth and slid the knife across his windpipe in one swift movement. The 'German' fell to the ground, his head hanging loose at a ghastly angle. The glass eyes of the uniformed dummy popped out to look at Liz and she stood and stared at them.

'Aye, but don't wait to apologize!' instructed Major Duncan.

Liz showed her determination to succeed in every part of the course – even in the lesson about survival in the wild, which included having to trap and kill food. Eight of the recruits including Liz, Matty, Colin and Suzanne stood in a group on the unkempt grass at the edge of a small field. A short thick-set game-keeper in cap and dirty gumboots towered over a small brown rabbit which struggled madly inside a grass net. Liz found herself almost tearful, hating even the thought of touching the poor animal which had been caught in their trap. The game-keeper raised his eyebrows in her direction, but she didn't move; she could not bring herself to step forward.

'Shall I do the honours?' Colin piped up helpfully.

'No, thank you,' she said curtly, mastering her feelings. 'I'll have to do my own dirty work out there.'

Abruptly she bent down and it took her a few moments to find a sharpish stone on the ground. She knew she must find the strength to kill, otherwise she would starve if left on her own. Quickly she raised her arm and brought down the stone . . . there was a nasty crack as it went straight through the rabbit's skull. For an instant she felt fulfilled rather than agonized by her action, but seconds later she reacted violently, and only just managed to get behind a thicket before her stomach heaved and she was as sick as a dog. She realized just how tough she would need to be in order to carry out this mission.

Colin and Matty were designated partners during a one-day training session with a canoe which Matty always remembered as an incongruous episode in her training. Despite the ominous package of explosives they carried, the sun and the lake worked their magic and both felt relaxed and released from the pressures of the course. Once they were launched on the water they began splashing each other with the paddles, tempted to behave as if on a picnic. When Matty enthusiastically rocked the boat, it tipped perilously and both were sobered by the thought that they might have over-turned it and scuppered the whole mission.

They looked towards the bank for the right spot to moor; having located a suitable place beside an old rotting boat-shed, they paddled gently towards it. Once there, Colin climbed out cautiously while Matty held the boat steady with both hands, a heavy brown-paper package resting on her knees. She threw him the rope and then carefully jumped out holding the parcel in her arms. Quickly he secured the end of the rope round a deep-rooted shrub on the bank.

Wordlessly the two recruits headed inland from the bank, following their instructions to the letter. They came through the undergrowth to a wooden hut and as usual Matty, who found it hard to be totally serious, irreverently voiced her thoughts on its similarity to an outdoor privy. They undid the neatly wrapped package and, on their hands and knees, laid an explosive charge and fuse under the hut. Matty stood up and brushed the dirt off her hands, watching Colin intently as he activated the fuse. That done, he sprang up and, grabbing her by the hand, led the way – slipping and sliding in the mud – back to the boat. They jumped in and Colin paddled energetically away from the shore. An explosion suddenly shattered the tranquillity of the still lake and Colin stopped paddling, allowing the canoe to float freely. Together they sat back, grinning at each other and watching the smoke and debris rise over the lake. Matty was chuffed to have succeeded and felt there was a camaraderie between them – something she had not experienced with a man before.

Matty found classroom sessions altogether less exhilarating than outdoor training, though she knew how important it was to learn military detail. She took notes furiously, trying to keep pace with Schweder's words, but was put out to find that it was constantly Pierre and Liz who were able to identify photographs immediately they were flashed up on a screen. She still had some difficulty in recognizing the subtle differences in the uniforms of the Abwehr, the German Army Intelligence and the Milice, French police collaborators. The higher ranks of the SS and the Gestapo were even more difficult to distinguish, as often they didn't wear uniforms but carried what Matty thought of as 'sneaky' metal discs which they only brought out when they wanted to identify themselves. Perhaps, she thought wryly, the Gestapo could only be distinguished by the curl of their lips!

Liz was horrified to realize how much everyday life in France had been affected by the Occupation.

'. . . and it is as well to remember that Frenchmen are not all on your side. They don't have to be in Milice uniform to be collaborators,' emphasized Schweder.

'It was a so-called Resistance worker who betrayed my family,' said Pierre bitterly.

Matty thought back to her own harrowing experience of France during the early days of the Occupation and for a moment she was far away from the slides and the lecture hall, reliving the fear generated by the presence of German troops.

She was relieved to be recalled to the present when Liz asked for her help in cracking the Morse code – that was one thing which Matty found it simple to cope with. Eagerly she threw off her disturbing recollections and became absorbed in explaining codes. The two of them walked out of the cluttered lecture room still engrossed in their discussion.

'One moment, Aimée,' Schweder called after her and, impassively, he handed Matty her notebook. Dismayed, she knew she had slipped up . . . and one slip in France would be fatal.

Liz was pleased to receive an invitation from Faith Ashley to have tea with her that afternoon at the training centre. She hadn't seen much of her since the original interview and was glad to have the opportunity of a chat, woman-to-woman, with someone like Faith who seemed to understand and care about her complicated family situation. Since she was not allowed to discuss her daughter with the other recruits, Faith was the only person to whom she thought she would be able to confess how much she missed Vicky, and how unsure she remained about her decision.

They sat at a table on the terrace overlooking the rolling lawns of Ettingley Manor, consuming tea and cucumber sandwiches. Despite the fact that she was gaining confidence through her success in the exercises, Liz felt a little nervous because she wanted to find out about the selection procedure from Faith. As they talked, it struck Liz that this encounter might be intended to test her real feelings on being separated from her daughter. But as she conjured up a vision of Vicky, her resolve was strengthened by the thought of Jack. She was absolutely determined that she would be chosen to go to France to do her bit – Jack's death would not have been in vain.

What Liz wanted to know was whether she could have a few days' leave to see Vicky, assuming she was selected to go to France. They chatted for a while and when she plucked up the courage to ask, Faith assured her that she would have at least a couple of days. Although reports from her grandmother confirmed that Vicky was settling down at boarding-school, Liz was still concerned as they had never been separated before. She showed Faith one of the child's drawings with Liz on one side and Vicky on the other.

'She always used to draw us standing together,' said Liz regretfully.

'What about your husband? Where does he fit in?' asked Faith.

'He's not very happy about me leaving Vicky to go out to work – he thinks I've joined the FANYs.'

Evading discussion of her own marriage, Liz asked Faith whether intelligence work had interfered with her family life.

'I was divorced years ago,' said Faith with composure. 'I share a flat with my sister now, but even she doesn't know what I really do.'

Liz was pleased that Faith had given her a rare glimpse of her private life. It was reassuring to know that she was not alone in having to keep secrets from her family. When Faith squeezed her arm softly, Liz was glad that someone understood what she was going through.

They sat in companionable silence in the pleasant afternoon sunshine. Some of the recruits were playing croquet on the lawn and Suzanne was showing Matty how to putt. The sound of their laughter drifted across to Liz and it seemed that on this agreeable afternoon Matty, who had always resented Suzanne's plummy tones, had overcome her feelings about class differences.

One evening in the dormitory the girls were occupied with different tasks. Liz was writing a difficult letter to Laurence, her brow furrowed as she sat at the little writing desk. Suzanne virtuously darned stockings and tried not to look at Thérèse who was cutting her fingernails on to the floor.

Suddenly Matty burst in, slamming the door behind her and they all jumped.

'Some of the blokes are going down the pub. Want to come?'

She looked round, beaming expectantly, but the response was unenthusiastic, the general consensus being that the pub was out of bounds. No one made a move to join her and Matty's face fell – she flounced out, slamming the door once more. There was a long silence in the room before Thérèse got up, carefully scooping up her nail-clippings and taking them into the bathroom.

Liz had sensed the rivalry that existed between Matty and Suzanne and worried about Matty's need to escape from tense situations. She guessed Suzanne might be about to comment on this, and was surprised when her approach was so tentative.

Suzanne looked up from her sewing. 'Celeste?' she said and Liz looked at her, glad to have an excuse to break off from her letter.

'There's something I wanted to tell you, while the others are out of the way.' She hesitated. 'I shall be off tomorrow.'

Liz's face was blank with amazement. 'Off where? Not to France?' Then she understood.

'I'm packing it in,' admitted Suzanne. 'I joined for the wrong reasons – I'd just had a letter from my fiancé breaking off our engagement and I didn't care about anything. Now suddenly I want to live. Do you think I'm a frightful coward?'

'Of course not.' Liz remembered Matty's observation. 'It sometimes takes more guts to say "No" than to go ahead.'

'That's how I lost my virginity!' Suzanne paused. 'It's all right to tell you my name now – its Felicity Hunter. Better not tell me yours.'

The local pub was busy when Matty entered. She was still in a bit of a huff over the other girls' refusal to join her, but cheered up when she saw how bright and jolly it was inside the bar. Looking about, she spotted Colin/ Cyrano sitting alone at a corner table, sipping a large Scotch. Matty waved at him to catch his attention and made her way over when he signalled for her to come and join him. She slid into the worn red velvet seat beside him and asked him for a cigarette. Happily he had some and they both lit up. Matty inhaled luxuriously, glad she had made the effort to come.

Once Colin had brought her a port and lemon they both relaxed and bantered happily, speculating about each other's lives and families. Matty rudely guessed that Cyrano might be an actor, given that he'd made such a daft choice for his code name. Her way of talking amused rather than antagonized him and he found himself opening up to her about his over-attentive mother and his father's death in a naval accident a month before he was born. He enjoyed his acting career and was happy to tell Matty about the last play he had been in, Rattigan's *French without Tears*.

'And now you're doing it *with* tears,' Matty commented and they both laughed. Matty looked at him questioningly.

'You married or anything?' she hazarded.

'I've escaped so far. How about you?' he returned.

'No one special. What's the point with a war on?' she said briskly.

He got the message and changed the subject. 'What did you do in civvy street?'

'Changed jobs every five minutes,' she laughed, then suddenly looked serious. 'I never knew what I wanted till this came up,' she said.

Later they were still chatting happily, having had several more drinks as the empty Scotch and port and lemon glasses lined up on the table proclaimed. Matty wanted to know how Colin had acquired his native French.

'Easy,' said Colin. 'We used to rent a house near Bragues for school holidays. Had a lot of friends in the French yachting fraternity too; I was always mad about boats.'

'That's why you chose the Navy,' Matty guessed.

'If I hadn't gone in for acting I'd have been a professional sailor like my father.'

They sat quietly for a moment.

'Crazy isn't it?' said Matty. It was more of a statement than a question.

'What in particular?' he asked.

'Here we are, all of us. Been so close these last weeks. And yet in a few days' time we'll say goodbye and won't even be able to swap names and addressess.'

'*C'est la vie*,' seemed to be the only possible response. It would be too dangerous for them to know each other's real names if they met in France; not knowing the facts meant that they couldn't give them away under any amount of pressure.

Pierre sidled up to their table just then. From the slur in his voice, it was apparent that he had downed a few. He leant over Matty's chair and talked to Colin.

'It is not fair, Cyrano. Why should you have Aimée to yourself?'

'Come and join us,' invited Colin.

Matty also encouraged Pierre to join them as she saw that this was a great opportunity to get a 'real' Frenchman to explain something she had been trying to work out recently. So once they had ordered another round of drinks she got the drunken Pierre to show her how the system of French food tickets operated.

Colin was aware that this was indiscreet and looked

about suspiciously at the tepid locals, wondering whether anyone might overhear them.

'Oh, for God's sake,' said Matty, irritated by his caution.

'We will speak French,' declared Pierre. 'Anyone who speaks French in this country is already one of us.'

He was well away, but Colin was concerned – one of the barmen seemed to be deliberately hovering within earshot. He decided it was time to leave.

In Colonel Cadogan's cramped office at the Baker Street HQ, Cad, Gil, Victor and Faith sat intently discussing the recruits: Cad formally ensconced behind his huge desk, Faith seated on a chair, Victor perched poised for action on top of the desk and Gil hunched on the chesterfield. They each had copies of different reports on the various candidates which they consulted while airing their respective views.

Cyrano – Colin Beale – met with unanimous approval: a good mixer, athletic and level-headed. Though Gil brought up the psychiatrist's reference to an Oedipus complex, Victor didn't seem to think that this mattered; the important thing was that he knew the Bragues area well and could be very useful.

Celeste – cautious, controlled, intelligent; there was some concern about her feelings on separation from her daughter, but a working knowledge of Area 3 and a useful contact from her schooldays tipped the balance, although Gil hammered on about not recruiting someone with a child.

'What does the psychiatrist say?' Victor cut in.

'For the umpteenth time, I will not base my decisions on what some pen-pushing quack says!' exploded Cad.

'Damn it, we'd never have sent Kit Vanston out there if we'd listened to the psychiatrist's report.' They agreed to send her.

One look at Aimée's report was enough to decide them and Gil expressed the general consensus.

'This says it all, doesn't it?'

It was left to Cad to break the news to Matty. Back at Ettingley Manor he found her in the lecture room and informed her of the decision.

'You're turning me down? She was horrified. 'You *can't!*'

Cad's face was grim. 'Major Duncan considers you'd be a security risk, and that's one thing I can't overlook.' He paused for a moment. 'You leave your notes lying around; you lose your temper easily; you talk too much – take the pub, for example . . . '

'But we were talking in French,' Matty argued.

'For crying out loud! Anyone could have overheard you and guessed what was going on at the Manor.'

Matty pleaded with him. 'Give me another chance; I came top in lots of the courses. You can't afford to turn me down – I know you need wireless operators urgently.'

But Cad was adamant, 'Do you know what it's like being a radio operator in Occupied France? It's probably the most dangerous job of all – the only one where you carry with you, all the time, tangible evidence of your guilt.'

'I'm not afraid of the risks . . . '

'I wasn't only thinking of the dangers,' he cut in. 'It's a very lonely job and you may go for days, weeks, without talking to a soul. And that's when boredom sets in. I'd say boredom was your worst enemy.'

Matty didn't want to hear what he was saying; she had worked so hard – they couldn't be failing her. She thought of her mother and of her cousins in France. She *had* to go.

'I can't just sit here and do nothing,' she begged.

Cad closed his file.

Later that day Liz and Matty were in the dormitory packing their things. Carefully Liz folded the garments she kept in her small bedside locker, placing her framed photograph of Vicky between two jumpers to keep it safe. She knew that she would soon be going off to France.

Matty still could not believe that she had been rejected. For the first time in her life she had found a job that was important and which she could do well. They couldn't do this to her! She just threw things into her case, too frustrated and angry to care. Shaking with anger, she snapped the lid shut. Sod them all, this was the most important thing in her life – why were they all so blind?

What would her future be? It was all a grim monotony of boredom; there was no point to anything.

Home in Devon, Liz, Evelyn and Vicky went out on one of their customary walks – Evelyn with a stout umbrella and Liz carrying a wicker basket in the hope of finding some early blackberries. Vicky clung to her mother's hand as they made their way past the tall blue delphinium flowers, out of the garden gate and up the path on the hill. The English fields spread out around them, unsullied by enemy invasion. This is what I'm fighting for, thought Liz; this is why I have to go to France.

Vicky refused to do her usual balancing act on the gate, preferring to stay at her mother's side although Liz urged her on.

'She's afraid you'll leave her again,' Evelyn remarked.

Liz looked round and back down the hill – at the house and the garden dotted with vivid herbaceous flowers, at the old swing hanging from the oak tree.

'I have to go on Monday,' she said slowly. 'They're sending me on another course.'

Matty was still in a bad mood when she got back to Stepney. She couldn't believe she was to be prevented from going to France – she knew that was where she should be. Albert didn't help much, showing his disapproval of her joining the FANYs. Nevertheless, they were pleased to see each other and Matty handed over the packets of Woodbines she had brought as a present. Aimée was as confused as ever and upset Matty by asking suspiciously where her husband Ron was – obviously believing that her absent daughter must have gone to join him at the front. Matty was very worried that her mother actually thought she had been in France already.

The days dragged by, with Matty bored and constantly on edge. At the factory the women had welcomed her back warmly, expecting her previous cheeriness, but soon left her alone when she went about with a permanently black face. She even rowed with Joyce. Albert spent as much time as possible digging on his allotment in order to avoid the sharp side of her tongue. Matty knew she was behaving badly and was conscious of the boredom which Cad had termed her worst enemy.

On the Friday a telegraph boy knocked at the door, his face appropriately solemn. Albert joined Matty on the doorstep as she opened the telegram.

'It's Ron, isn't it?' he said, but in reply she simply flung her arms around his neck.

'They want me, they want me!' she cried.

'And so they bloody well should,' he retorted caustically, concealing his pride and relief.

Two days previously Cad had called an emergency meeting in his office. Word had come through from Kit Vanston that their ring in Area 3 had been infiltrated. The agent planted in the docks had been killed and Kit was having to lie low, only able to transmit messages via a wireless operator 100 kilometres away.

Cad was extremely worried that Kit was feeling the strain, not least because he had already had five months of it. It was up to them now to send out a back-up team. He had already decided that Colin Beale, with his naval training, would be the perfect man to send to the docks. Also, he suggested, Elizabeth Grainger would be useful as the courier they required, since she had a safe house in Bragues with her old school-friend. The one problem was a wireless operator; all the best ones were in the field and the new recruits were still training.

'Better get on to the school and see if there's anyone sufficiently advanced,' proposed Gil. Cad and Faith exchanged glances.

'Faith's already been on,' said Cad, 'and there isn't anyone. The only name that came up was Mathilde Firman; she did very well on the course and they recommend we reassess her.'

Both Victor and Gil looked unimpressed – wanting someone they considered totally reliable for this particularly dangerous job – but Cad had made up his mind that Matty had learnt her lesson and she was the best operator they had available.

*

At the Parkgrove Mansions HQ, preparations for a full briefing and departure were under way. Over informal cups of tea in a sparse reception room, Cad was instructing the selected trio on the task ahead. Colin learned that he was being posted to the docks to monitor naval activity. Liz was to act as liaison between Gregoire, the leader, and Colin and Matty. Matty was to have the crucial role of maintaining communications between France and London at all costs.

'It's no use pretending that it won't be hazardous work for all of you,' warned Cad, 'but it is work that is absolutely essential to the war effort. Our instructions have come from the top.'

All these solemn pronouncements seemed less memorable to Matty than her final briefing when Victor Travussini helped her and Liz to devise and memorize their respective cover stories. Meetings in other parts of the flat had driven them into the bathroom for privacy. Victor, looking slick and darkly attractive, sat ceremonially atop the black lid of the lavatory while the two women perched on the edge of the bath.

'My name is Celeste Sarasin,' recited Liz. 'I was born in St Etienne in 1914. I am in Bragues visiting my old school-friend, Claudine de Valois. I have been recently widowed – the RAF bombed my home, killing my husband, so I'm none too fond of the British . . . '

Matty began to reel off her piece, still trying not to giggle at the sight of Victor directing activities from the lavatory seat.

'I'm a district nurse, which allows me to travel over a wide area . . . ' She broke off. 'Major Travussini, you've been on missions. What's it really like?'

Victor considered. 'A battle, a game of wits, a chance to find out about yourself.'

A number of things needed attention before the operation began. Hair, clothes and jewellery had to be changed to the French style. Matty was disappointed to find that she would have to wear drab, inconspicuous clothes rather than her favourite bright colours, although she grudgingly admitted there was a certain amount of chic in the cut. The changes were more traumatic for Liz, who found to her horror that even dental work was different on the Continent; her small silver-coloured fillings were mercilessly drilled out and replaced with gold ones.

Faith took Liz to Cartiers to have her wedding ring replaced by a more suitable one. The elaborate velvet decor of the discreet back room was comforting, but Liz felt a distinct pang when they were compelled to cut away her own wedding ring; she had not removed it since she and Laurence were married. Faith smiled sympathetically as she picked up the severed gold band.

They returned to Parkgrove Mansions and found a free reception room where Faith took out her notebook before resuming the conversation.

'You do realize that once you're out there there can be no regular form of communication with your relatives?'

Liz nodded. 'But if you could send my mother a note periodically – just say that I'm well in Scotland – and she'll pass it on to Laurence.'

'And if you're captured?' Faith asked.

Liz took a deep breath. 'Only tell them if you have definite news that I'm dead. I've lodged my will with my bank . . . and one other thing – I shall be writing a whole lot of postcards for Vicky. Would you mind posting them to her at regular intervals?'

Faith looked at her, conscious of the fight going on within her.

'It's not too late to turn back,' she said, but Liz shook her head.

'Laurence and I talked a lot about the kind of world we wanted our daughter to grow up in. People like my brother have given their lives to fight for that world and I feel that if I don't carry on that fight, his death will have been for nothing.'

Faith felt that the mood was getting too emotional and assumed her businesslike manner again.

'Let me have the postcards before you go. And now, if you'd like to go home for a day or two . . . we'll notify you when we're ready for standby.'

The call had come and Liz and Matty were installed for the night at the Hotel Albion. Liz sat in her room reciting her cover story as though it were some kind of mystical incantation. Finally weary, she knelt by her bed and the incantation became a prayer.

Meanwhile Matty had not been able to stand the gloom of her bleak hotel room. Taking her keys, she swept through the door and out into the streets of Bayswater in search of a cinema. She didn't really care what she saw, she just wanted distraction. At last she found an Odeon, bought a ticket and slipped into a seat near the back of the auditorium in the middle of the main feature. Hardly concentrating on the screen, she looked listlessly around and spotted a soldier sitting on his own in the row in front of her. Suddenly he looked round in her direction; their eyes locked and with practised ease he vaulted over the seats to sit beside her. They chatted in undertones and very soon left the cinema together.

In the dim light of her hotel room, Matty wound her arms round the soldier's neck and kissed him hard on the

70

mouth; his lips opened and urgently she pushed and bit. As they kissed she tore open his shirt, pulling it off. She needed to escape from this terrible lull, the emptiness of this moment before she left for France. She ran her hands hard down his back and over his buttocks, feeling the tremor in his body and the surge in his groin, then pushed him backwards so that they fell entwined on to the narrow bed. Their hips ground together and Matty unbuttoned his trousers. Her skirt had already worked its way up around her waist.

Arching her back in reaction to the young soldier's deep penetration, Matty squirmed and pushed, clawing at him savagely with her nails – feeling him with every inch of her body in her desperation to free herself from the unbearable tension of the last few days. The more she tried, the more difficult she found it and she bit his neck in frustration. He sensed what she needed and, forcing her back on the bed with an abrupt jerk of his hand, moved down her body and kissed and stroked her until at last she came. Then he climbed back on to her and they writhed and pounded until he stopped, out of breath. They lay panting, sweaty and twitching.

'I'm sorry,' said Matty.

'Sorry!' He was surprised.

'I used you,' she explained.

'Feel free any time,' he joked, then looked at her and saw how serious she was.

'Why tonight?' he asked.

'I just needed to take my mind off something.' Matty was hesitant.

'If you were a bloke, I'd say you were going on active service.'

Early the following evening Colin, Matty and Liz

71

assembled at the holding station, ready for their final security check. The three of them stood around, slightly self-conscious in their unfamiliar French outfits, though Colin liked his scruffy working clothes – a comfortable change after his stiff Navy uniform – and Liz looked highly fashionable and half wished Laurence could see her now. Their open cases were laid out for inspection on a large trestle table and Faith and Cad busied themselves dispensing papers and French money. A security man walked around each one of them carefully checking every pocket and tuck, every facet of the correct French 'look'. He pulled out a photograph of Vicky from Liz's handbag and gave it to Faith.

Faith and Liz looked at each other. Liz had not thought it would be particularly risky to take the picture with her – after all, it could be of a niece or godchild, anybody. She could see that Faith was not happy about it and in fact tried to be as kind as she could, but as she put the photograph into the buff-covered file containing Liz's papers and closed it with finality, Liz felt as if the lid of a coffin had been sealed between her and her little daughter. She gasped with pain.

'I'll keep it safe for you,' Faith said sympathetically.

Liz decided she should ask Faith to sort out something which had been bothering her before she left it too late.

'May I ask you something? It's about Vicky . . . ' she began. 'She went down with whooping-cough before I left . . . ' Here she broke off, misconstruing the look of concern on Faith's face. 'It's all right, I've had it. I'm sure it'll run the normal course, but . . . '

Faith immediately reassured her that she would be in touch with Evelyn and get a message into France via Aimée as soon as she could.

The ordeal seemed to be over when Cad finally

handed out three little boxes. Colin knew what this was and nodded, tucking his away securely in a pocket. Matty did not at first realize and only understood when she opened her box and saw the tiny cyanide pill. She handed hers back to Cad decisively.

'Do we have to take them with us?' she added, obviously not intending to.

'I can't force you,' he replied gravely, 'but at least I hope you will accept these.' He turned and took three small packages from Faith and handed them round.

'A small gift from all of us at HQ,' he said.

They opened the gifts and were touched to find silver compacts for the girls and a silver cigarette case for Colin – a thoughtful send-off. Liz opened her compact and read the inscription inside the lid: '*Bonne Chance*'.

CHAPTER 3

It was dark, strange and almost wild; the tall trees around the clearing where the Lysander had landed tossing against the sky, the long grass blown flat and empty of all life. Liz had never had such a confusing welcome to France. All the training and expectations she had built up were confounded by the random nature of their arrival . . . it seemed bungled.

Liz did not feel very encouraged by events on their arrival in France. One man had come out of the forest to meet them. He was a swarthy, heavy-set figure who had greeted them with scant courtesy, introducing himself as Maurice, leader of the local Resistance. He had been most put out to find two women in the party – told to expect one woman, it had not occcurred to him that the radio operator might also be female. Matty had asserted that she was in fact the wireless operator and he was not at all impressed. In addition to this, Gregoire, the head of their own group in the area, was conspicuous by his absence. Maurice had led them through the woods in the darkness and Liz was horrified to see a sinister group of people coming towards them. In the darkness all three had thought they must be German, and for a terrible moment it seemed they had been betrayed. Liz's fear changed to fury when Maurice explained in an off-hand way that it was only some of the villagers come out to welcome them, word having spread about the drop. If this was the level of security they could expect they were unlikely to last long here, she thought.

'What about the curfew?' she muttered under her breath, worried and angered by this confusing state of affairs.

'Never mind that, what about the Germans?' Matty was louder and sounded more forceful.

But Maurice simply got impatient with them and turned on Matty angrily. 'You standing here bellyaching isn't going to improve matters.'

After that they were silent and just followed him through the darkness.

Later Matty and Liz sat up in the hay-loft of a barn they had been taken to by Maurice. After supper Colin had gone off home with the Frenchman; he was to stay with Maurice's family at their farm just outside Gouloncourt until members of the Resistance cell were able to find him other accommodation nearer the port.

The girls sat talking quietly atop a couple of thread-bare blankets that were laid out on the straw; they both lolled comfortably in their petticoats, having removed their clothes and hung them over some of the low beams to prevent them from creasing. It was typical of Liz, thought Matty, to insist on this careful management of their clothes; for some reason she was convinced they would look more French if they looked neat. Matty, on the other hand, had reverted to feeling, and even being, her French self from the moment they had arrived with Maurice at the barn and he had given them large hunks of crusty bread and thick garlicky vegetable soup.

The spiciness and oil had awakened familiar feelings, though she did admit to Liz that she could hardly believe it.

'Used to be the same when I visited my grandparents. First night, I'd keep pinching myself. Then I'd wake up to the smell of fresh bread and start to feel French again.'

Meanwhile Liz had been scraping the mud off her shoes with a stick, aware of the possibility of the Germans conducting shoe inspections. Bits of congealed mud kept falling on the blanket and she swept them off with the side of her hand. Her mind wandered to the conversation at supper.

Over the soup Colin had been stroppy with Maurice, wanting to know exactly what had happened to Gregoire and where he was. He wasn't even sure he could trust any instructions Maurice gave them; they had no proof that he was genuine and he had already managed to let the whole neighbourhood know of their arrival. This kind of criticism had only caused an argument.

'We can't afford to waste time quibbling amongst ourselves.' Liz brought them to a halt and Matty was impressed, if not amused, by the impact of her head-girl tone.

At least, thought Liz as she passed the shoe-scraper to Matty, insisting that her shoes needed the same treatment, we have got our instructions from Maurice and we can get on tomorrow morning, find Gregoire and begin serious work. Maurice had arranged for them to cycle in the morning to Carpet-La-Fontaine, a village forty kilometres away where Gregoire was staying. When they reached the village they were to go to the churchyard and find a note hidden in a large crack in the third grave on the left from the gate. The grave belonged to the Choulac family and was used regularly by members of the Resistance as a letter-box. All this Liz repeated over and over in her head, making certain the key words were committed to memory.

Looking round at Matty, she found that she was still earnestly and messily dislodging mud. So far so good, pondered Liz, the only immediate problem being the discovery that Matty could not ride a bicycle. When it became apparent that one of the machines Maurice had arranged for them to use was a man's model, Matty had voiced her hope of perhaps finding a bus instead. Unfortunately Maurice had assured her there was no bus going that way and had found her an alternative bicycle. She would simply have to make the best of it, and Liz hoped that this would not delay them unduly in reaching Carpet-La-Fontaine and Gregoire.

Seeing the church spire ahead, Liz got off her bike and, holding the handlebars securely in her left hand, turned to face the road behind her while waiting for Matty to catch up. She could just make out Matty struggling along on her bike in the distance, doubtless muttering expletives. At last she caught up with Liz on the dusty road and was relieved to see the church ahead of them. They set off again, but this time wheeling the cycles.

Liz felt conspicuous as they entered the main square of Carpet-La-Fontaine where whitewashed buildings with red-brick tiled roofs surrounded the cobbled square. She glanced about her nervously, anticipating hostility and perhaps surprise from the locals at seeing strangers, but passing villagers appeared to accept them as French women. Matty was at home immediately, nodding and smiling at the odd passer-by. Noticing a café with tables outside it on the other side of the square, she thought longingly of the delights of a large cup of strong coffee. She looked at Liz to see how she might react to this proposition and gauged that it would be wiser not to risk it. Liz was obviously intent on getting to the church as quickly as possible.

Two German soldiers approached them – swaggering along, Matty noted bitterly, as if they owned the place. These were the first Germans they had encountered and the sudden reality of what lay ahead startled them. The girls turned and pretended to be looking at a display of vegetables outside one of the little shops on the square. Liz tried to calm her nerves, deliberately diverting her attention sufficiently to gaze at the lavish display of onions all tied together on strings. She wished she could buy some for her mother, who loved to use them in her cooking; they had all but disappeared from the shops in England. The thought of Evelyn composing her daily menus with the cook in their flagstoned kitchen helped Liz to cope with her fear. Matty already knew what it was to be stopped and searched by German soldiers and she tensed as they passed by, giving the women only a cursory glance. Relieved, they made their way more cheerfully to the church.

'I'll go in. You keep watch,' Matty said when they arrived at the church gate.

'Third one on the left . . . Choulac,' Liz reminded her.

'I know!' Matty snapped, slightly on edge; the tension was returning now that she had to carry out the first part of their instructions. She left Liz and went in through the gate, turning left once inside and looking for the grave marked 'Choulac'. She saw it almost immediately, but seeing that a woman was tending the grave next to it she passed by and busied herself reading the long inscription on another grave. The graveyard was old and romantically overgrown with long grasses and clusters of small, brightly coloured flowers.

Outside Liz sat stiffly on a bench near the gate, pretending to read a French paperback, her hands shaking so much that she could hardly have focused on the words even if she had wanted to. She kept glancing at her watch. Hearing the sound of footsteps approaching, she looked up to see a man walking by – very ordinary-looking, she thought, dressed in scruffy peasant clothes. Then she saw his curly red hair and started with alarm; collecting herself she looked again and could see his face, and the freckles. While she sat there flustered, he had walked by seemingly oblivious to her – taking the road marked 'Bessinville' out of the village, she noticed. I *know* that man, she thought, groping to remember the detail.

The woman at the grave next to the one marked Choulac knelt down and crossed herself and began to pray. Matty watched her impatiently, trying her best to look nonchalant – wandering up to other graves close by, reading the inscriptions and looking at the displays of flowers, some in pots and some planted neatly. One grave had an evergreen wreath hanging crookedly from a corner of its gravestone. She looked back towards the Choulac grave and watched the woman cross herself again before getting up and moving off towards the gate.

After a quick glance around, Matty went back down the narrow muddy path and over to the grave. 'Jean Pierre and Marie Choulac', she read, 'much loved husband and wife'.

Hastily she found the crack in the side of the stone and, having taken the precaution of another glance around, removed the slip of paper from inside it. Still standing at the graveside with head bowed like a mourner, she read the instructions carefully, then committed them to memory by repeating them over to herself without looking at the paper. She tore up the paper into little pieces and buried them in three small holes she made in the earth covering one of the other graves. Aware that Liz had now been waiting for quite a time, she hurried towards the church gate to find her.

By the time Matty joined Liz both girls were on edge and managed to upset each other by saying the wrong things.

'Sorry, only . . . ' Liz was the first to apologize.

'I know – a bit different from training, isn't it?' Matty was apologetic too.

'What are our instructions?' asked Liz, decisively cutting through the backchat.

'We're to take the Bessinville road,' began Matty. Beginning to wonder if the man she had recognized could be an Englishman and perhaps was Gregoire, their leader, Liz's mind raced while Matty continued relaying the instructions.

'There's a farmhouse about a kilometre on and Gregoire will be there. We're to say we're his cousins from Lyons. Come on, we'd better fetch our cases.'

'Look, Aimée,' Liz cut in, 'I don't think we should arrive at the farm together.'

She couldn't explain to Matty why she wanted to go on ahead, but she thought it was best not to tell her that she might have known Gregoire in England. Secrecy still had to be maintained as far as possible for the sake of security. Matty was not keen to be left behind and could not make out what had got into Liz.

'Give me five minutes or so, then you follow on,' Liz ordered. 'I have my reasons.'

*

80

The farm was old and walled; dogs and chickens created inordinate amounts of noise and smell. As Liz wobbled and bumped over the cobblestones of the inner quadrangle of the farmyard a large black dog rushed barking towards her, then stopped in its tracks as a boy of about twelve materialized, trailing a pail of chicken feed. She got off her bike and left it leaning against a wall. With a smile and a nod to the boy, she crossed the yard and found herself at what must be the kitchen door. A fat middle-aged woman of peasant stock appeared and ushered her in once she had explained she was one of the 'cousins' from Lyons. The woman introduced herself as Clothilde.

'Your cousin is here, Gregoire!' Clothilde shouted up from the foot of a flight of stone steps.

'Come up!' came the equally loud reply. Liz thanked her and climbed up the stairs.

Once at the top and a trifle out of breath, Liz found herself in a small attic room with a sloping roof and two miniature windows. There wasn't much in the way of furniture; a table under one of the windows, with a wash basin and floral china jug alongside, comprised most of the room's contents. Gregoire closed the door behind Liz and then turned into the room to face her. This was the leader Victor had briefed them about.

While they stood weighing each other up, neither saying anything for a moment, Liz had the chance to take a proper look at him. Yes, it *was* Kit! He looked older than she remembered him – wrinkled around his piercing, intelligent blue eyes – but after all he would be getting on for forty, she guessed. It must have been years since she had met him at Oxford with Jack, where they had shared an enthusiasm for rowing. She looked into his eyes and saw an intensity there – she realized at that moment that he was not pleased to see her and was going to react just as Jack would have done.

'Jack Woodville's sister!' He paused. 'Liz, isn't it?' Without waiting for a reply, he went on, 'What the devil are you doing here?'

'Same as you,' she countered.

'But you're a married woman with a child. What the hell's Cad thinking of?'

Liz was angry at his reaction, but remained cool.

'He wouldn't have sent me if I wasn't up to the job,' she replied evenly.

He stared at her impatiently. 'And how will I face up to Jack after the war if you end up in the hands of the Gestapo?'

'Jack's dead,' Liz cut in and Kit's face changed, his jaw tightening. He gripped the back of the chair, for a moment unable to speak.

'When?' he asked quietly.

'February. He was shot down in a bombing raid,' she answered.

'And you think this is what he'd have wanted?'

Kit was all for sending her back if he could but Liz dug her heels in; she was in Bragues, doing this job because she wanted to, and he would have to put up with it. Finally he gave up and enquired after the wireless operator; they were supposed to have arrived together. Liz explained she had thought it best under the circumstances to meet him first. He assumed the operator to be a man and she found herself having to disillusion him before Matty's arrival.

'God in heaven!' Kit sighed as it sank in.

'She was the best on the course,' Liz added.

'They sit there in London, shifting their coloured pins around. Do they know how long wireless operators are lasting out here, on average?'

'Then it's time we upped the average, isn't it?' Matty, to Liz's intense relief, had appeared in the doorway.

By the end of the afternoon Kit had supplied Matty with her radio and sent her cycling precariously off to Rocheville, where she would find her first safe house. As she cycled, she thought of all the instructions she had received during her training. This would be her first chance to make a transmission at her 'sked' – the regular prearranged time for transmission. She had had the codes drummed into her and for the last few weeks had dreamt in the 'Q-code'. As she pedalled, she thought: QSM – repeat last remark; QRS – send slower; QRV – I am ready; QSL – I acknowledge receipt of message; QRT – stop sending . . . Kit had told her she would not be able to transmit from the farm as it was too dangerous, and that once she had done her first sked from Rocheville she would have to move on every couple of days in order to avoid German detector vans. Matty had been horrified to discover that Rocheville was a good twenty-five kilometres away. She had, somehow, managed to cycle forty already that day. But Kit was unsympathetic.

'Start complaining when you're doing a hundred a day,' he advised.

After seeing Matty off, Liz went back into the farmhouse, worrying because she had just let slip to her that she already knew Kit.

'That buggers up their effing rules!' Matty had laughed. She was not particularly surprised, for after all everyone else on the course had been at the same schools and universities.

'Least no one from *my* old school's likely to turn up,' she concluded.

83

The girls had hugged each other warmly before Matty cycled off.

Liz made her way up the staircase to the attic room, where Kit joined her soon after with two steaming cups of ersatz coffee. In the quiet of the little room, he began to go over with her the problems involved in carrying out her job as courier. He explained that he needed her to carry out dangerous errands he would normally have been able to do himself. Now he had to lie low, no one must know where he was living.

'There's been a lot of activity in the docks recently,' Kit confided, 'and it's essential we find out what they're up to. We've already lost two men trying to do so.'

Liz discovered that she would be moving to Gouloncourt, to a safe house with her friend Claudine de Valois, though this had not been confirmed yet. Part of her job would include regular liaison with Aimée and Cyrano and this pleased her, as it meant she would always know that they were all right. So far as she could see, everything was working out well, though Kit was more hesitant and did not seem to trust anyone. She asked how well he knew Claudine – had she been working for the Resistance all along?

'No. She's arranged the occasional money loan for us and once passed on some valuable information from the German officers.'

'She must loathe them,' said Liz.

Kit went on to tell her that security had doubled in the area since the Germans had appointed a new Abwehr chief, Colonel Krieger. She would have to watch out for him and, unfortunately, for other enemies who were more difficult to discern – the French collaborators. Liz leaned back in her chair, cradling her nearly empty coffee cup in both hands as she watched Kit's tired face.

'Fear breeds collaborators,' he stated, and she sensed that he was suffering not only from long exposure to tensions, but also a wearied acceptance of the fact that not all the French were on the same side. After a short silence, he went back to discussing briskly the work they still had to do,

'I'll need you to search for suitable landing sites and to organize reception committees when there's a drop. We're short of supplies. As soon as Aimée's made contact, we can start building things up again.'

When Liz asked whether there was any possibility of getting another cup of coffee Kit smiled, his face suddenly younger again, and went off downstairs to arrange it.

Several cups of muddy coffee later, Liz was feeling refreshed and recovered from the morning's activities. She and Kit remained sitting at the table, idly studying some maps of the area which had been printed on to silk squares so that they could be easily concealed as scarves. She arranged them in sequence on the table-top in order to check her route to Gouloncourt, and she recalled her briefing. There was Bragues, the port town dominating Area 3; she and Kit were deep inland, almost into Area 2, while Claudine lived two-thirds of the way to the coast. She glanced at her watch.

'Aimée should be nearly at Rocheville,' she considered.

Kit spoke gently. 'Take my advice and don't get close to anyone. It makes you vulnerable.'

Liz looked at him and saw he had meant it. He must have seen that she and Matty had become friends – but how could you do this job and not become close to those you trust? She wondered how badly he had been hurt, how many of his friends he had seen fall into the hands of the Gestapo . . . and whether that explained his re-action to their arrival.

By the time Matty reached Rocheville she was ex-hausted. The cases strapped to the back of her bike made the unfamiliar cycling even harder. She got off her machine and stood holding on to it, panting for a minute or two, then slowly trudged on up the road until she reached a small house on the outskirts of town, where she parked her bicycle and went up to the door and rapped. There was no reply and she tried again. Some time went by before an old woman came to the door and looked at her very suspiciously. Matty tried the pre-arranged sentence to no avail; the woman would not let her in and made as if to close the door. Not knowing what else to do, Matty pleaded on.

'He is expecting me,' she insisted.

In a cracked voice the woman finally told her, 'You are too late. The Gestapo have already been and they have taken my son and his wife for questioning . . . '

Matty found herself standing alone on the doorstep, the door firmly slammed in her face. She was terrified – were the Germans watching the house? Forcing herself to move away, she knew she had nowhere to go although she walked on wheeling the bike and not allowing herself to look back. She was certain she would be arrested at any minute. Finally she turned a corner into a steep path running between two houses where she stopped, leaned her bicycle against the wall and looked back. No one seemed to be following her.

She waited for her heart to slow down to its normal rate, convincing herself that she must go on into town and try to find a place to spend the night from which she would be able to transmit. She was painfully aware that if she did not find somewhere very quickly she would miss her first sked. As she pushed her bike down the narrow cobbled streets of Rocheville she passed a few people, including a German soldier, but no one took any notice of the dirty travel-weary girl. Too tired to go any further, she entered a rather shabby hotel, no longer able to consider whether this was safe.

A severe middle-aged woman in spectacles behind the reception desk allocated her a room and Matty insisted on carting her own luggage. It was a tremendous relief to get upstairs and into her room, where she plonked down both cases and sat on the bed, kicking off her shoes. A quick look at her watch told her it was very close to the time for her first evening sked. If she did not transmit, London would not know of their safe arrival.

She looked about the room for a suitable place to hang the aerial. Over the window she discovered a narrow ledge and was just working out how to climb up there when there was a knock at the door. Startled, she shoved her radio case under the bed.

'Mam'selle?' it was the voice of the receptionist from downstairs.

'Just coming,' she called and opened the door to find the spectacled receptionist standing there with a towel over one arm. She looked uneasy, Matty thought.

'Excuse me. May I come in?' she said, and then whispered, 'It's important.'

Matty let her in and the receptionist closed the door securely behind her. She spoke urgently.

'I don't know who you are, but you must leave first thing in the morning. And if you were thinking of transmitting from this room, forget it! There are Germans on either side of you.'

At first Matty could not understand how the woman could not understand how the woman could know what she was up to and denied any comprehension of such an intention, but the woman was impatient with her.

'That is a radio set, isn't it?' she said briskly, pointing under the bed. She had no time to discuss Matty's cover story and obviously did not believe that Matty was a district nurse. District nurses did not carry false identity cards like the one Matty had shown her downstairs.

Having delivered her blow, she allowed herself a quick smile of encouragement to Matty and then departed.

'Sod!' Matty breathed audibly. 'Sod, *sod*!' Everything was going wrong. There was no way she would be able to get a message through to London tonight.

At a receiving centre in a seaside town on the South Coast of England, Lois Mountjoy sat tuning up her radio receiving set ready for Aimée's first sked. She turned a large side knob and found the correct frequency, then sighed and remained seated, hunched over her desk, drumming her fingers and waiting.

Eighteen-year-old Lois had been on the radio training course with Matty and admired the older girl. She had elected to be Matty's 'godmother' as they had got on splendidly. This relationship meant that Lois would receive all Matty's messages and thus would be able to build up a dialogue over the airwaves and to decipher her messages even when there was interference. During the training they had begun to feel close, though they came from widely differing backgrounds. Lois, sheltered daughter of a country vicar, had been determined once away from home to learn the ways of the world.

Matty was the perfect source – her anecdotes about her racy past taught the impressionable young Lois a vocabulary that would have shocked her father considerably.

Now Lois, a pretty fair-haired girl with healthy pink cheeks and an earnest expression, slid on her headphones and looked at the time. She juggled the knob around gently, searching in case Matty came in slightly off the prearranged frequency. But although she concentrated hard she found nothing and began to worry about her friend; it was jolly frustrating simply having to wait. The time of the sked passed and she realized despondently that no message was going to come through on this occasion.

The cock crowed at dawn and Liz woke with a start, wondering where on earth she was. She dressed hurriedly and climbed down from her attic and out into the farmyard to find Kit had beaten her to it and was already washing at the pump. Following the directions she had gleaned earlier from Clothilde, she clambered through the kitchen garden in search of the privy, which made itself evident by its smell. She had forgotten the indelicacies of French rural sanitation.

When she got back to the pump, Kit was still washing, the band of muscles in his arms moving rhythmically as he soaped his neck. His bare skin gleamed above his khaki work trousers and a sprinkling of freckles spread from the nape of his neck down his back. He bent under the pump to wash off the soap and straightened up, turning towards her. He caught sight of her and waved and Liz saw the damp red-gold hairs matted on his broad chest and the well-defined pectoral muscles.

He called Liz over and began to give her instructions

for immediate action that morning. His directions were specific. She was to get to Lasseron station, which he had already shown her on the map, and take the second turning into Le Boulevard des Lombards. Here she was to meet a man named Picolet who ran the import-export business at No. 50.

'He's about my height, balding,' Kit elaborated. She was to collect a package containing forged documents and then catch the number 3 train to Cairon-St Marguerite. Once there she would easily spot a garage painted red and yellow and was to ask the owner, Bruni – who was tall with dark curly hair and aged about thirty – to hold five hundred litres of petrol at their disposal. He handed her a large bundle of notes for this purpose. Liz secured the notes in the waistband of her skirt and repeated some key words, a method of memorizing instructions which she had found to be successful.

Liz had to stand for an age in the queue at the little station at Carpet-La-Fontaine. In front of her a small child hanging from her mother's hip flung her grubby rag-doll to the ground. Liz bent and picked it up for her. The mother thanked her and apologized for the child, who promptly threw the doll down again.

'Don't worry, they all do that at her age,' Liz smiled.

'You have children yourself?' the woman asked. Liz paused.

'No,' she replied. She had passed the first test of her new identity that morning.

German voices shouted loudly, disrupting the relative calm of the station. Two heavy German policemen stood barring the exit from the ticket office.

'Have your papers ready,' one of them ordered and

the people in the queue began to get out their papers. Liz, seeing no way out, rummaged through her bag to find hers as one of the policemen moved forward, checking each person's papers cursorily as he went. The other remained squarely in place. Liz clenched one fist, her other hand damp round her documents; this was the second test of her assumed identity. When the German reached her, he seemed to scrutinize her papers more closely than the others. Would he be able to detect the forgery, worried Liz? With a curt nod he handed the papers back to her. She had passed the second test.

Since she had been unable to transmit from the hotel the previous night, Matty had cycled off down a country lane looking for a suitably secluded spot from which to contact Lois. She pedalled painstakingly, gazing into the bushes, not noticing that she had drifted over to the left-hand side of the road. In her absorption she only distantly heard the sound of an approaching vehicle. All at once the driver sounded his horn and Matty swerved violently and then fell off into the road. The vegetables hiding her radio spilled out of the front basket and scattered across the ground.

'Are you all right, miss?'

Matty picked herself up to find that it was Colin.

'Cyrano!' she fumed. 'I might have known . . . maniac!'

'You can talk,' he said through clenched teeth.

'I cycle round half France and it has to be you who runs me over,' she spat.

'Damn lucky it *was* me! Do you realize you were riding on the wrong side of the road? Anyone could have told from a mile off that you were English!'

Matty stood in silent horror, furious with her own stupidity. 'God, I could kill myself,' she exclaimed.

'Not until they've sent another wireless operator!' he retorted.

She looked at him and they began to laugh in spite of themselves, but a little hysterically.

He helped her to pick up the damaged bike and put it into the back of his truck. Maurice had fixed him up with a job in transport – delivering stuff to the docks, he told Matty. She explained that everything had gone wrong and she was going to have to transmit from behind a bush.

'Is that safe?' he queried.

'Nothing's bloody well safe, is it?'

Despite the fact that they were not supposed to meet even in private unless it was vital, Colin felt he wanted to help Matty. He did not see that it could do any harm. Also, with her dark hair in disarray and her face white with anxiety, she was rather attractive.

Together they found a conveniently overhung spot beside a field and Matty burrowed in with her radio, preparing to set it up for transmission. Colin remained on the narrow road with his truck, anxiously keeping a look-out as Matty fast became engrossed in her work. She sat in the prickly grass with her earphones on, carefully tuning her set. But it was not to be. Colin heard a loud mooing sound and, looking up from his position in the cab of the truck, saw an old man driving a herd of cows towards Matty's field. This is turning my heroic act into a farce, he thought as he leapt out of the cab and hurried to warn her.

In the truck once again, they drove slowly down the road hoping to find another possible spot further on.

'Bloody cows,' Matty muttered under her breath with

frustration. They continued driving for a while in silence.

'Have you let Gregoire know about your safe house being blown?' Colin broke through the tension.

'I left a note in one of the dead-letter drops.'

'He may have arranged somewhere else then,' suggested Colin.

Matty was sceptical as to whether he would have received the message, but heartened by the possibility they set off, following her directions to see if there was an answer. In the cab she noticed how different Cyrano looked; he had absorbed the mannerisms of a French worker and really taken her in when she had seen him earlier.

She jumped out of the lorry at the appropriate spot in a densely wooded lane and hunted about for a particularly thick-trunked tree. One stood out from the others and she hurried round to the far side of it to find a crevice in the wood. And yes . . . triumphantly she tugged out a note, then ran back round the tree and made a cheery thumb-ups sign at Colin before joining him in the cab.

Through his attic window, Kit watched Liz push her bike up the bumpy track and into the farmyard. He went down and out into the forecourt to greet her, relieved to have her back in one piece.

'You took your time. Did you miss the four-forty?' he asked briskly.

'No, it was derailed. Explosives on the line.'

'Where?'

'Outside Alainville,' she informed him.

'It wasn't our lot.' He was extremely frustrated. 'Must

have been the Free French again. God! Why the hell can't they let us know what they're up to?' He paused and looked at her. 'Are you all right?' he asked more calmly.

Liz felt fine; she had followed the instructions closely and found the whole thing perfectly straightforward. They walked side by side through the pleasant early evening light into the farmhouse.

Up in the attic, Kit brought out a dusty bottle of red wine and two glasses and they sat at the table drinking companionably. Sipping her wine, Liz thought about Matty. Kit had told her of the note he had received and she just prayed that Matty had collected the reply safely and was by now installed in a safe house.

As they leaned back peacefully in their chairs, Liz noticed that Kit looked far more relaxed than she had seen him before and took it as a compliment to her day's success. She felt his attitude towards her had changed because he was now convinced she was capable of doing the job.

'You'll be moving on to stay with your friend Claudine in Gouloncourt at the end of the week,' he said.

'It will be odd seeing her in these circumstances,' Liz mused. She had not seen her friend since the summer before the war, but that should not matter – time had never made any difference to their friendship; they had always just picked up where they had left off.

Kit sipped his rough wine and reminisced with Liz, remembering the last time they had seen each other at a picnic by the river in Henley – quite a contrast to their present situation. Jack had been there, glamorous in his straw boater and white blazer, playing with Vicky – then just a toddler laughing with delight as he spun her around yelling for more. Laurence had not been there;

he had been working as usual, remembered Liz, though his absence had not really spoilt the joy of the day.

'And your wife and children were there,' said Liz. 'Where are they now?'

'They're not. They were killed in the blitz.'

'Oh, Kit . . . ' Liz searched for something to say but it was far too terrible for words and she could only touch his hand. He understood what lay behind the gesture but withdrew his hand, concluding abruptly, 'Don't say anything. There's nothing to be said.'

They sat on quietly finishing the bottle of wine as the room grew gradually darker. Neither of them got up to turn on a light.

Colin pulled up his truck in a side street outside a modest pre-war block of flats with a dismally peeling façade. He and Matty got out and went round to the back to unload Matty's bike, then they looked over at the building.

'Apartment 32,' she recited unenthusiastically.

'Want me to come in with you?' Colin offered in an attempt to cheer her up.

'No, you've done enough,' said Matty as she wheeled her bike towards the building. Tiredness had begun to make her feel irritable; he had been kind, but now she was hoping to transmit to London she did not need him any more.

Colin watched her climb the stairs, admiring her courage. He had never known a girl like her before.

It was quite a long haul to the top of the apartment block, where Matty finally discovered No. 32. She opened the door with the keys the caretaker had given her and dumped her radio-case inside on the floor. Then she crossed the poky bed-sitting room to the window and waved down to Colin that she was all right. He waved back, then turned his keys in the ignition and drove off along the street; Matty watched from the window as he rounded the corner and disappeared down the main road.

She turned back into the room and went over to make sure the door was securely locked. Opening the radio-case, she took out the aerial and then looked about, considering where best to put it. Finally she decided she would try to hang it out of the window again, as this did seem the only way to guarantee a reasonable connection. Carrying the aerial, and dragging behind it the thin wire which was attached to the radio, she pushed open the window and looked out and up. From here she could see the cracked metal guttering just above her and the roof beyond. Leaning out of the window as far as she dared, she swung the wiring round like a cowboy with a lariat and managed to hook the aerial securely on to the guttering. Glancing down, she froze. Two thuggish members of the Milice were standing in the street below and for a long moment she could not even breathe. She sighed with relief as they began to walk away down the street and, glancing hastily at her watch, walked over to the radio.

She sat quietly on the narrow single bed with the radio-case open beside her, checking her coded message. She turned the dial to the right frequency and tapped in her signal . . . then she waited.

Simultaneously Lois sat ready at her post in the receiving centre. Earphones firmly in place, she tuned her dial and listened. A row of operators in cubicles all down the room sat in similar poses, all listening intently to every crackle on a variety of frequencies. Lois tuned back and forward on either side of Matty's frequency, her brow creased with total concentration. She glanced at her watch, retuned to the exact wavelength and waited again. Miraculously Matty's signals began to come through and Lois listened intently and began to take down the message. She stopped momentarily, looking puzzled, then cut in on Matty's transmission to ask her to start again. The signals stopped abruptly and then began once more, this time a little more clearly. Again Lois took down the message, but still with some difficulty. It was a slow process.

Half an hour later Lois got up from her seat, rushed breathlessly up to her supervisor's desk and handed over the messages.

'Here, sir,' she puffed. 'The reception was terrible!'

Having finished her transmission , Matty went back to the open window and tugged at the wire hanging down from the guttering, hoping to dislodge it easily. However it would not unhook, remaining obstinately aloft. Just at that second a detector van with tall aerial protruding screeched to a halt in the street. Matty stared aghast, then desperately yanked her aerial down and out of the guttering with one mighty tug. She pulled it back inside and secured the window as German soldiers piled out of the van and ran towards the building.

Faith had sat through the evening with Cad in his Baker Street office, drinking cup after cup of coffee. While he worked through a generous supply of cigarettes, Faith had only puffed nervously on one. The butts mounted up in the onyx ashtray – a present from Cad's wife Helen –

which was placed strategically half-way between the two in the centre of the large desk. The phone rang at last and Faith waited tensely while Cad answered the call. Finally he hung up and looked at her.

'She's made contact.'

'Thank God,' breathed Faith.

'Yes,' said Cad. 'Now we're back in business.'

CHAPTER 4

Clothilde stirred a big cauldron of thick, bubbling vegetable soup on the range, expertly adding herbs and seasoning. With the delicious smells filling the kitchen, Liz found it hard to concentrate on her day's briefing with Kit. They sat at the dark wooden kitchen table downing tumblers of purple Bessinville wine, a rather potent brew. Liz was fortifying herself for her departure to Gouloncourt where she was to make contact with Claudine.

Taking down a generous ladle from where it hung on a rack near the open brick fireplace, Clothilde began to serve out portions of soup into pottery bowls. She carried two bowls over to Liz and Kit at the table and then took out a crusty golden baguette from the oven and put that out as well. Liz watched Kit tear off a hunk of bread and dip it into his soup, and followed suit. There was a silence as they consumed their lunch eagerly. Finally putting down their spoons, they sat back replete and smiled at each other.

'Do you remember the directions from Gouloncourt station?' Kit asked. Immediately their relationship had resumed its businesslike form and Liz felt flickers of nervous excitement as she repeated the details.

'By the station there'll be a check-point, probably due

to the Free French bomb on the railway line. Turn right by the butcher's, through the market, and the estate manager's office is in the street behind the church. I wonder if that amazing pastry shop is still on the same street? Claudine and I used to haunt it constantly.' She broke off in a trance of remembered *tartes*.

'But can we depend on her?' worried Kit.

Liz was defensive. 'She was my best friend, surely that counts for something?'

Kit still wasn't totally reassured; after all, he argued, their lives depended on this woman's loyalty to the Resistance. If she turned out to be an informer – and there were many of them – it would be fatal. The recent billeting of the new Abwehr Colonel Krieger and his men to Claudine's château left ample opportunity for collaboration.

'That's unfair,' she protested. 'Claudine will hate them all the more for taking away her home.'

'Perhaps, but we just don't know.'

'I *know* Claudine has always been utterly reliable.' Liz wanted to convince him that she was right. She had known Claudine for so many years – they had shared their most personal secrets and there was no question of lack of confidence. She wanted Kit to understand her and agree, but his face held no such response and she was shocked at his inability to trust.

Matty had succeeded in pulling in her aerial through the window. As the German soldiers piled out of the car below, she desperately coiled the wire and crammed it into the suitcase with the wireless. Then she pushed everything level and tried to snap the clasps closed – blast, it had stuck. Holding it together, she slipped out of the front door of her apartment and opened the boiler-cupboard door. Quickly she stuffed the case into an assorted heap of builders' rubble beneath the boiler, and as she heard the soldiers banging on the doors of the floor below, she wedged the door shut again. Then she sprinted back across the landing into her room and gently closed the door behind her.

By the time the soldiers reached her apartment she had thrust her head under the tap and was busy lathering soap into her hair. When the knock came she called out for them to come in and two soldiers entered; she watched them through her soapy hair and saw that they were satisfied. They had seen nothing of her face before they left and would not recognize her again.

The van drove away and she sank down on the bed. The violent fit of shivering was not caused by her wet hair.

Liz free-wheeled down the steep hill to the small town of Gouloncourt. Plodding up towards her was a horse and cart – she realized she had not yet seen a car on her journey. Spread beneath her were rows of streets; it was as peaceful as on a saint's day. She passed the cart and braked at the bottom of the hill, then got off the bike and looked around her. An old man in a rough serge shirt and patched trousers sat in a kitchen chair on the pavement; his walnut-wrinkled face stared at her impassively as slowly he raised a clay pipe to his mouth and drew in a mouthful of smoke. She hesitated, then nodded a good morning to him and walked past.

Claudine de Valois emerged from the sitting room at the back of the estate manager's lodge, looking immaculately chic despite wartime privations. Pearl earrings relieved the severity of a well-cut navy suit. Her hair was drawn back into a charming chignon and her face was lightly made up to emphasize her distinguished features.

In the small room overlooking the street, Claudine had created a bookshop from what had originally been the office of her estate manager. Between the shelves laden with novels stood a couple of customers, browsing, and Colonel Heinz Krieger.

The tall, handsome German bowed formally and clicked his heels and she greeted him courteously. She always felt that she had at least to be polite to the Germans. They had a brief exchange of niceties, Krieger scrupulously treating her as the lady of the manor. She felt it was important to keep up a good relationship with him in case there was a need to plead for one of the local boys involved with the Resistance.

Krieger commented that the week had been very uneventful and that Gouloncourt would prosper under his direction. 'You can trust me, Madame de Valois,' he said.

'We don't have much option do we, Colonel?' replied Claudine, smiling.

'No, you don't, do you?' Krieger responded smoothly.

He lingered in the shop while Claudine continued to be as charming as she could manage. She was becoming used to this most annoying habit of having to spend the afternoon in the company of German officers. Didn't they have any work to do in the afternoons, she wondered? And how dare they insist on taking up so much of her time? In normal circumstances she had never had to be so conciliatory to such crashing bores. Claudine picked up a pile of books and carried them through to the sitting room.

Liz walked into the shop and the door tinkled as she closed it. She looked about her. Instead of an office there were stacks of books. Suddenly a German officer appeared from behind a tall bookshelf and she tried to conceal her dismay. Not having known that the estate manager's office had been turned into a bookshop, her first instinct was to turn and leave, but quickly she decided that would be too suspicious and turned to face him instead.

'I was expecting the estate manager's office,' she said hesitantly.

'You've just arrived in Gouloncourt?' questioned Krieger.

'From Rossans . . . ' Her cover story came to her lips, despite the confusion she was feeling. Where on earth was Claudine, she wondered desperately. The letter should have reached her by now, warning her of Liz's arrival and of her new identity.

At this moment Claudine walked back into the shop and when for a fraction of a second she failed to recognize her friend, Liz realized that her letter could not have got through. Quickly she embraced Claudine, kissing her on both cheeks. The French woman responded warmly and Liz knew that somehow she must communicate her false identity to Claudine in front of the German.

'I can't tell you what a journey it was from Rossans! But why didn't you tell me about this?' As she spoke and gestured round the shop, Claudine rapidly recovered her customary poise.

'My dear, this is only my first week here. You remember all those hundreds and hundreds of books we always had around the place?'

'Who could forget?' said Liz. 'You always said you could open a library.'

Claudine gestured around her with both hands and the two girls laughed delightedly. They could hardly stop – it was such a blessed release of tension – but the laughter also rang true because the girls were pleased – and Liz relieved – to see each other. Krieger was not suspicious, though he listened to them anyway, enjoying the reunion for what he thought it was.

Claudine was the first to speak again, realizing that it was vital for their stories to dove-tail.

'I was going to write, but you know how it is. I'm just so busy these days,' she said, with a hint of a question in her voice.

Liz took up the story.

'You always were busy! But I did write. Didn't you get my letter?' she prompted, gripping Claudine's arm warningly.

'Not yet. Colonel Krieger, you must attend to the postal service. I'm afraid it's just as bad as it was under Reynaud . . . ' She spoke lightly and then gestured politely towards Krieger, explaining, 'This is Colonel Krieger. He's in charge of . . . well, just about everything round here as far as Bragues.'

'Celeste Sarasin, Colonel,' Liz introduced herself quickly.

'Charmed, Madame,' he replied, bowing courteously, without a hint of humour.

'We've known each other for ages, since schooldays in fact,' Liz continued, trying to reassure herself that she and Claudine were managing their public reunion quite well.

'Did you have braces on your teeth?' Krieger addressed Liz and she was thrown by the oddity of the question. Was this some kind of test?

'I did, actually,' she managed to stammer, sounding as put out as she felt.

'I was telling the Colonel yesterday that I never wore them as a child,' Claudine explained, coming to her rescue. 'Celeste was just as pretty, but somehow her parents decided her teeth had to be straightened – and just look how wonderfully she turned out.'

Liz smiled as Claudine flung her arms round her once more, this time with a genuine warmth and emotion and less surprise. The old friends continued to hug each other for a while, happy to be together and delighted to have decieved Krieger so far.

He coughed slightly with embarrassment at this prolonged display of affection and the two disengaged themselves.

'The Colonel and I were just about to have a drink,' said Claudine. 'Take off your coat and let's sit down. Sophie's back there somewhere.'

Liz sensed the warning in Claudine's tone; Sophie, her long-term domestic servant, was unlikely to comprehend the situation without explanations. Claudine was torn in two directions; she should speak to Sophie, but she did not want to leave Liz to face Krieger alone.

'What we need is a jolly good gossip. The Colonel will be bored rigid, I'm afraid.' This she added in the hope that he might take the hint and leave, but he was becoming a little suspicious.

'Very unlikely, Madame de Valois. I shall be intrigued, I'm sure.'

Bastard, thought Liz to herself, as they moved into the living quarters behind the shop.

Looking back on it, Liz thought the drinks session with Krieger – which must have lasted for anything up to an hour – was the most excruciatingly awful experience she had been through – definitely the worst since she had arrived in France, if not ever. Sophie, looking fatter than ever in her black dress and starched apron, had handed round little glasses of cognac and Liz had been petrified every time she entered the room lest she reveal her real name. Sophie, for her part, was wildly confused about the whole thing and looked it, remaining almost totally silent.

They had played what was ostensibly a game of cat and mouse: Claudine and herself trying to keep the conversation light and bubbly and Krieger interjecting the occasional – and on the surface, harmless – question just to keep them on their toes. As far as Liz could tell, he must have been aware of Sophie's open puzzlement and the growing tension. However, she could not fathom exactly how much he had worked out, or quite how intelligent or stupid he might be. During their conversation she had successfully passed on her complete cover story.

'And after Lausanne?' Krieger asked, as if unaware that he had overstayed his welcome.

'The Sorbonne,' Liz replied.

'The Sorbonne?' said Krieger. 'You were clever girls,' he added, unpleasantly emphasizing the 'were'.

'Oh, we never did a stroke of work. Complete mystery to me how we ever passed an exam,' Liz rejoined lightly.

Claudine broke in, 'Celeste, honestly! You were a terrible swot.' She looked at Krieger, hoping that he would be distracted by her schoolgirl mood. 'Always had her head in a book, that one.'

'Claudine, what do you mean?' Liz teased. 'Every time I sat down to work, she would be sweeping me off to go swimming or dancing or to parties . . . '

'That was your real education,' insisted Claudine.

'You had no discipline?' suggested Krieger.

Liz had been tempted to tell him just how much self-discipline they did have, considering how well they had behaved all afternoon, but she had restrained herself and continued with a girlish giggle, 'We stayed with Claudine's aunt. She was . . . a little deaf.'

'A little? She wouldn't have noticed the entire Military Academy marching upstairs!' added Claudine saucily. She felt drunk with exhilaration – they were getting away with it; she had been so politic with the Germans since the Occupation, but now Liz was forcing her to throw caution to the winds.

'And did they?' asked Krieger.

'It's true she was a little deaf, but we never took advantage of her, did we, Celeste? she bantered.

'Oh, never,' Liz responded.

Krieger continued subtly to question Liz, while she gave him as little information as she could, allowing herself to join Claudine in a hysterically frivolous mood.

Liz could not wait for this appalling man to go. She was dying to catch up on lost time with Claudine, and he had continued with his banalities for ages. But there was nothing she could do to bring the charming get-together to its conclusion. Krieger could feel the tension and his instinct was to investigate; he was in charge – only he could end the encounter by leaving. It must have pleased him in a sadistic kind of way to prolong their 'show'.

At long last the German left, buying some books on the way out for which he politely insisted on paying.

Once they had shut the shop door securely behind him, the two women flopped down together on the sofa and Claudine hugged Liz with relief.

'I nearly died on the spot when I saw you!' she exclaimed.

All her fears were now rushing to the surface and Liz

knew she would have to explain quickly and calm her friend down. Quietly she told her about the letter which should have come by courier; something must have happened to the courier, she supposed.

Claudine began to chide Liz for endangering her, unable to believe that she had just behaved in such a foolhardy way. Her life since the Occupation had been a series of delicate balancing acts so as to stay elegantly poised on the fence. Now Liz, who had always been the one to play safe and issue the cautions, had appeared in a mad escapade which was totally out of character. There was only one explanation – Jack must have put her up to it. She suggested this to Liz.

'Why should he?' retorted Liz. 'Why couldn't *I* have wanted to do something for France?'

'Don't you realize what it's like out here?' argued her friend.

'Well, I'm here,' stated Liz, 'because I want to be. Not for Jack – for me . . . Jack died in February, shot down in a bombing raid.'

'Oh, Liz, I'm sorry.' Claudine broke off and she and Liz sat for a moment without speaking. She remembered the riotous weekend the three of them had spent in Paris; Liz and Jack together were willing to dare anything. They had danced together, a handsome pair who had attracted a lot of attention. In the middle of the dance floor Jack had begun to clown around, embarrassing Claudine, but Liz had relaxed into the 'routine' and soon they were the only people dancing before an appreciative audience. Claudine knew that her friend must feel as if she was only half a person without her brother.

Claudine apologized, remarks tumbling over each other: she was not sure who Liz was supposed to be; she had not expected anything like this; she had been shocked to see her.

'My name is Celeste Sarasin,' Liz recited helpfully. 'I'm a part-time teacher from Rossans . . . My husband Raoul was killed in a British bombing raid in September 1941 . . . '

'Liz, please,' Claudine interrupted. 'Stop it – tell me about Vicky; how big she must be! What is she now? Five? How could you leave her at that age?'

'We were married for seven years,' continued Liz, 'but we had no children . . . ' She broke off suddenly and flung off her assumed character.

'Claudine, I need your help,' she whispered urgently.

Colin and Armand – a Resistance activist and second-in-command to the Communist Maurice in the Bragues area – stood on the road leading to the quayside of the Bragues docks, shovelling a tall heap of coal into dirty sacks which were rapidly changing colour to match the coal. As the men filled the sacks, they slung them on to the back of a small lorry. Having significantly reduced the coal heap in size, they stopped for a break to clear their throats of coal-dust and, lighting up their cigarettes, sauntered a little way along the quay. They could now observe the activity across a stretch of water, on the quay that was fenced off and used by the German Navy. A ship was being unloaded by crane and Colin could see the huge unmarked cases stacked and well guarded by soldiers with rifles. Other soldiers in shirtsleeves had begun to load these crates on to a lorry.

'Can't see exactly what it is, can you?' asked Colin between drags.

'Ammo?' suggested Armand. They continued to watch as surreptitiously as possible. Armand pulled his cap down over his face and stamped out one cigarette before lighting up another. There was nothing remarkable about him; he had short darkish hair, easily forgotten features and was of medium build and height. For this reason he was very well suited to working for a secret organization – no one ever noticed him particularly.

'Could be ammo,' agreed Colin, watching the continued action. 'Hello, that bloke's for it! Ah, smoking. Maybe you're right – looks like it must be ammo.'

'Can you hear some kind of a machine?' asked Armand.

Action on the quayside continued for some time and they noted that a staff car drew up and several officers got out. Another lorry which pulled up ready for unloading appeared to contain sand.

Colin pulled out a pair of field-glasses and moved further along their quay, hoping to get a better angle. Alarmed at this blatancy, Armand left him and went back to his appointed job shovelling coal. A German soldier approached Armand and he hastily offered the man a cigarette to distract him, but the man shook his head and moved off purposefully towards where Colin was still leaning against a wall looking into the forbidden area. When the soldier reached Colin he roughly yanked him round to face him. Colin was eating a hunk of baguette and ham and appeared shocked by the sudden intrusion. The soldier gestured angrily for him to get back to work and he did so, looking sullenly resentful as he swallowed the last of his food in a couple of bites.

As they resumed work, he whispered to Armand, 'It's sand. They've got a cement-mixer over there – going full blast too. So . . . ammo, concrete. What does all that add up to, do you reckon?'

It took very little imagination to deduce that some kind of building work was in process.

Colin considered that with this latest gem of information he had a good excuse to pay a call on Matty that evening. He disregarded Gregoire's instructions to meet as little as possible, and to make contact only through the dead-letter boxes, telling himself that the information merited immediate transmission. In reality, however, he needed to unwind with a friend he could talk to. He found her at Apartment 32, just about to begin transmission of her evening sked. He gave her the new message and she coded it before replacing her headphones and tuning into Lois. She transmitted from a precarious position, both she and the radio set being balanced on her narrow bed.

Leaving her to it, Colin went through a doorway and out into a little side room which housed a small sink with a single tap and running water. It could almost have been called the bathroom except that there was no bath and no lavatory but, as all the British agents had grown to accept, these were small luxuries they generally had to do without. He spent some time doing the best he could – with a rough towel, a restricted flow of cold water and no mirror – to clean off the filthy coal-dust that clung to him. What blackness did come off was soon deeply ingrained in the towel.

At last Colin emerged, feeling a bit fresher after the wash.

'Come on, Aimée; it's been nearly half an hour,' he said urgently.

Matty looked worried as she tried to get the last of her message across quickly – she had told him about her near miss with the detector van the last time she overran her sked. However, both she and Colin knew this was not an episode to be repeated; one minute too long could very likely herald a tragedy.

There was a final burst of activity on the machine from London, then Matty signed off and pulled off her headset with a flourish.

'Well done, Lois! You're a gem,' she commented brightly before turning to Colin. Shocked, she regarded him speechlessly, then finally she found her voice.

'My God! You pig!'

'Eh?' muttered Colin, thrown. 'Come on, I was just reminding you . . . '

'My towel!' she screamed hoarsely. 'My *only* towel . . . what have you done?'

Colin took off the towel from where he had draped it round his shoulders. It was totally blackened with coaldust.

'I'm sorry,' he apologized and Matty saw from his expression that she had overreacted. All this being shut up on her own was having a bad effect. Colin was out and about living what appeared to be a normal life, working and meeting other people, whereas she was limited to two trips a day to dead-letter boxes and a prearranged weekly session in the local café waiting for other messages.

Gallantly Colin offered to take her out to find something to eat. He could see that she needed a break and knew it was important for her to keep level-headed. Although it was a risk for them to be seen together, he thought they both deserved a change. Matty packed up her radio eagerly; she loved going out.

As they walked to the door, Colin picked up Matty's coat and draped it round her shoulders. Then he opened the door and stood back chivalrously for her to pass through before him. As he watched her swan by, he realized that he was not simply doing her a favour – he was actually looking forward to spending time with her.

He was about to turn off the light when he noticed her notebook, containing all her codes, lying on the floor. He caught her arm, twisting her round so that she could see it.

'Oh, God!' she exclaimed as she went back to pick it up. 'It'll be the death of me.'

Matty carried her radio-case out of the apartment, with the notebook duly returned to its proper place inside. After locking the door, she went over the secrete the apparatus in its hiding-place under the boiler. She closed the cupboard door firmly and turned back to Colin, and the two began their descent of the endless stairs.

'Deliveries of ammunition including torpedoes, Colin thinks,' Faith read out to Cad from the scrawled, decoded message on its flimsy piece of paper. They sat late that evening in his office, happy at last to be achieving some results with their team.

'Submarines, do you suppose?' mused Cad.

'Sounds like U-boats to me,' said Faith. 'Inspection by high-ranking officer . . . deliveries of sand, cement-mixer busy . . .'

Cad picked up and read a report from Area 2 which described barges on the canals carrying gravel, moving up towards Bragues. Sand, gravel and cement-mixers meant concrete, and concrete probably meant fortifications.

'They're obviously strengthening the place,' Faith concluded, but what all this was actually for they could only guess. As always they needed more information, and as always it would be a long time coming. Cad felt inadequate; it was frustrating and they got no help from any other government spy network, though even the PM probably knew bugger-all anyway.

As usual the pair sat long into the night deliberating, going over and over pieces of information and fitting the puzzle together in what seemed like a million different combinations.

Faith had often had to contemplate the fact that her agents were involved in complicated work which would take months to complete. Now that Liz was in France, she admitted to herself that she was particularly concerned for her. Looking down again over all the accumulated messages, Faith acknowledged that Area 3 was strategically vital; the Bragues port could be the starting point for an invasion. It was painful to think of Liz caught in the fighting.

Matty found herself being hauled up the steps of the imposing Gouloncourt town hall, now Abwehr headquarters. She wriggled a little, trying to get the lieutenant who had arrested her outside her apartment to relax his hold on her arm. She glanced up at the huge red banners with their white circles containing black swastikas which hung on either side of the high entrance, and gritted her teeth. They weren't going to frighten her; she had been picked up during a series of routine checks on people new to the area.

The lieutenant pushed her into Colonel Krieger's office and pointed to the hard-looking upright chair facing his desk. Matty went over to it and sat down. Defiantly she stared straight into the eyes of Hitler, whose portrait hung directly opposite her over the desk. She was at the nerve centre of Nazi operations in the area and it terrified her. The lieutenant sat in Krieger's own comfortable office chair and examined her identity card carefully before looking up at her.

'You moved into your present flat fifteen days ago?'

'Yes,' she replied, controlling her fear by concentrating on answering him convincingly. He picked up a pen and began to take notes.

'And before that?' he asked.

'In Rocheville. I trained in Charentes; I was posted to Rocheville in June.'

'So I see,' said the lieutenant, looking at her papers. Would he notice they were forged, she worried? Laboriously he wrote some more notes.

'Look,' she interrupted, taking her courage in both hands, 'will this take long? Only I have a number of patients to visit this morning . . . '

Her voice trailed off as the office door opened and Krieger entered, clearly in a bad mood. He limped over to his desk and gestured dismissively with his arm for them to leave him in peace.

Matty stood up, unsure what to do, while Krieger and the lieutenant proceeded to argue heatedly in German. Krieger, as far as Matty could tell, seemed particularly angry with the lieutenant, which she hoped might bode well for her. Finally he left the room, leaving her alone with the nervy Krieger. Standing uneasily, she watched him wince with pain.

'Are you all right?' she asked.

'Unfortunately, the answer is *no*.' He rubbed his shin.

'How did it happen?' she ventured.

'Minor accident this morning,' he muttered.

'I'm a nurse.' She saw her passport to get out of this place. 'Can I look at it for you?'

He did not make any particular move to reply, but Matty bravely decided to take matters into her own

115

hands, not stopping to consider the possible consequences if her advances proved unwelcome. Going
round to his side of the desk, she saw that his trouser-leg
was torn and quite a lot of blood was coming through the
hole below his knee.

'That's going to be painful,' she said sympathetically,
looking up at his contorted face. 'The ankle's already
started to swell. I can dress the wound, but you should
have a cold compress on that ankle.'

Krieger allowed her to dress his ankle and Matty
fussed around, soaking the bandage in cold water before
wrapping it tightly round the wound. She mentioned in
passing that she thought the lieutenant had gone through
all the necessary questions with her, so she would have
to leave soon. She saw that Krieger would be more
difficult to fool than the lieutenant and was frightened
that he would see through her assumed identity.

'It's just that I've got all these appointments, you see,
and I wasn't expecting to spend a day here.'

With all her kindly attention, Krieger seemed to have
calmed down. He stood up gingerly to test her handi-
work.

'Wonderful,' he concluded, pleasantly surprised to
find that there was little or no pain when he put his
weight down on the injured foot.

'Good,' responded Matty.

'You say my lieutenant questioned you before I
arrived?' he said, sitting down again.

'He said it was just routine.'

Krieger handed back her ID card and papers.

'For the moment. But there have been outbreaks of
senseless vandalism and nobody is free of suspicion. It is
really quite pointless to take on the might of the German
Army.' It occurred to Matty that his tone was rapidly
deteriorating into a far less convivial one; she hoped he

was not going to change his mind.

'Perhaps you could make the point on your rounds?' he continued.

'I don't think any of my patients are capable of things like that.' She tried to sound convincing.

'I think you know what I mean,' he remarked, his tone cool but with a hint of menace. He was nobody's fool, Matty realized nervously; she hoped she had not gone too far.

'Perhaps you would care to come and look at the wound again in a day or so,' he said, looking her up and down in a manner which would have been lecherous had he not been so formal. She nodded in reply and, taking this as a dismissal, picked up her case and left the room. Krieger looked after her with a puzzled frown, thinking that there was something slightly wrong about Aimée.

Liz spent the night at Claudine's and the next morning went off to report to Kit. In the bright morning light she was glad to leave Gouloncourt's narrow streets behind her and cycle up the hill towards the open countryside. Swathes of lacy white flowers filled the ditches on either side of her, and the tall popular trees receded towards the horizon. The road was deserted; this was the France she knew.

Turning off the road, she followed a lane which finally led to the farmhouse. Her bicycle bumped over the sun-dried ruts and as she got closer she could see Kit's red hair as he worked in the yard, scattering feed for the chickens. Liz waved and was surprised how eagerly he came to greet her. She dismounted and wheeled her bike over the cobbles and into the yard, propping it up against the shed wall.

Kit's worried look changed to a smile as he gave her a

quick hug, his bare arm warm against her shoulders. She felt embarrassed by this show of affection and blushed. Turning towards the house, she hurried on ahead of him into the farmhouse kitchen.

Once more Liz sat at the big wooden table while Kit stood at the stove expertly heating up a pan of roasted acorn coffee. As she began to tell him about her meeting with Claudine, he took the pan off the stove and poured the coffee into two bowls on the table.

Kit broke in to her account, explaining that almost as soon as she had left Maurice had rushed over to let him know there had been an accident, which was why the courier had never reached Gouloncourt – the lad had been knocked down by a German lorry.

'There was nothing I could do to warn you that you were not expected,' Kit concluded.

She reassured him that she had been in no danger; Claudine was not a collaborator, even though she did have constant contact with Krieger. But her old school-friend had said that she could not provide a home for Liz for more than one night. Claudine was worried that Krieger would be suspicious, and Kit agreed that there was probably something in that – it was very risky.

But Liz was disappointed in Claudine's reaction, for she had anticipated that she would be whole-hearted in her support of the Resistance. When they were growing up Claudine had been the one with the looks and the exciting boyfriends – always taking risks. Now her best friend was letting her down. Liz forced herself to acknowledge that she was asking a great deal. The penalties for failure were dire, and naturally Claudine wanted to protect herself: the Occupation was having its effect on everyone.

'Where else could I stay?' Liz asked.

'Well, we could find someone from Maurice's group, but I don't think that's a solution,' he said thoughtfully. 'I don't want all my agents being reliant on the same group – there could always be an informer.'

'Where can I stay, then?' she wondered.

'Anywhere else will take time to arrange. Can you convince Claudine to have you on a temporary basis?'

Liz thought it was possible that Claudine would agree to this. After all, she had been helpful enough to say she would try to find her a part-time teaching job in Gouloncourt.

She was thrilled when Kit handed her a letter from England that had arrived in the previous night's drop. It was from Vicky, saying that she had got over the whooping-cough, though the medicine tasted horrid. For a moment, holding the letter, Liz left her assumed identity way behind and allowed her love for her daughter to flow back.

To her surprise Kit was impatient with her mood and made her tear up the letter and drop it into the stove.

'Destruction for security,' he reminded her.

Liz could not understand why he was being so brusque; his tone upset her. Then she realized his attitude must be due to the reminder, through her family, of his own wife and daughters. Suddenly she was all concern.

'Sorry. I know how you must feel – your wife and family – it was tactless of me.'

'You have nothing to apologize for. You didn't drop the bomb,' he said bitterly.

Now that she had raised the subject she wanted to give him the chance to talk about it and asked how it had happened.

Kit told her how his family had been killed while on

their way to visit an aunt's house in London. A bomb had dropped on the underground station as they emerged, killing them instantly and scattering their bodies so they could never be recovered and identified. Liz thought of Jack's plane exploding into a ball of fire.

'Kit, you've got to talk about it. It's only talking that makes it bearable.'

'No,' he made a tangible effort. 'I'm Gregoire and you're Celeste and we're here to do a job and if we let our personal feelings get in the way . . . '

Liz broke in, saying something she had been thinking about for a while; 'That's what we're fighting against, that awful anonymity . . . ' She began to try to put into words everything she felt about the effects of the war and the Occupation – the change in Claudine, the threat of the Germans on the streets, the sullenness that seemed to have affected everyone. Kit tried to calm her down. He had been in France so long that he was beginning to take for granted the double standards which the Occupation had imposed on local people. He made her see that the changes were not permanent; they were both fighting for what was best in France, and what was best in the French responded to that. Looking at him, she thought how strong he was and how much he had had to endure since the war began. It was men like him who would win the war for the Allies.

They heard the sound of an engine drawing up outside – it was Colin's truck. When he came in to join them, grimy with coal-dust, Liz saw from his face that something had happened and was instantly convinced it must be to do with Matty. Hundreds of awful possiblities flashed through her mind, but Colin very quickly explained that he had just heard that Matty had been taken to Abwehr headquarters for questioning. The concierge at her apartment had insisted that this was routine for newcomers to the area.

Kit's concern, however, was primarily for the radio. Liz wanted to find out more about what had happened to Matty, but instead Kit insisted that she knew no more than was absolutely necessary. He told her to go on with her work and make the next pick-up, also to go back to Claudine's to discuss accommodation.

Liz went disconsolately out into the farmyard, climbed on to her bike and rode off out of the gate. A few minutes later she was overtaken by Kit and Colin in the truck.

The men had prepared themselves for the worst and Kit was totally practical about the possibilities – radio operators never lasted long. Colin let his emotions show in his harrowed expression; he cared about Matty. They drove in tense silence and Colin parked some distance from Matty's apartment building.

Led by Colin, they climbed warily up the stairs to apartment 32. When they got to the top landing Colin went straight over to look in the boiler cupboard where the radio set should have been, but there was no sign of it.

'Are you sure that's where she kept it?' asked Kit. Colin's horrified face was enough reply and in whispers they began to discuss what action they should take. They both jumped as the door behind them opened, expecting Germans . . . but they were face to face with Matty. Colin looked as though he had seen a ghost, then he hugged her.

'I heard somebody outside,' whispered Matty. 'I was terrified.'

*

Claudine was engaged in trying to arrange her books into something resembling order, but she was distracted by the constant chatterings of Thérèse, Krieger's frivolous young mistress. At a glance one could understand what her chief attractions were for him – she had curly blonde hair precariously restrained by ribbons, her large breasts swelled under her flounced silk blouse and her shapely long legs were encased in expensive stockings. Claudine would never have chosen even to talk to this type of girl normally. Thérèse had been ostracized by many of her neighbours and this made her miserable, which in turn annoyed Krieger. He had encouraged Thérèse to spend time with Claudine, who now had to control herself and behave civilly as she did not want to antagonize Krieger.

Thérèse flitted around amongst the piles of books, looking like a top-heavy butterfly, wondering aloud about her new dress and whether Heinz would like it. Claudine found it hard to take these speculations. No one else in the area had any choice in their new clothes and she could only despise Thérèse for her method of getting things.

'It's so unfair,' moaned Thérèse. 'My mother's windows have been broken again – it's not as if I'm doing anything wrong! I think people are horrible.'

Claudine could understand only too well the sentiment behind the act. 'It must be very difficult.' Once more she had to suppress her true feelings – it was becoming a way of life.

It was four hours since Liz had cycled away from the farmyard. The curfew was past and she was miles from anywhere on the road between Evrechamps and Gouloncourt. She stood in the dark unable to comprehend that on top of everything else her bike was packing up on her. By now she could hardly see the road ahead and the steadily falling rain had penetrated her clothes. She thought she must still be anything up to twenty kilometres away from Gouloncourt.

Pulling her bike under the doubtful cover of a large tree, Liz tried to decide what to do. She had spent the afternoon riding around the countryside from village to village and farm to farm, delivering and passing on messages which had been initiated by the new drop. Now she felt as miserable as hell and her tired brain seemed useless in resolving her situation. I must get on, she thought, but she was still hesitant. The only safe place seemed to be Claudine's – it was far too late to get back to Kit and the farm – but she had promised not to return there for another night. She took out her torch and carefully examined the damage to the bike; it was no good, she would have to leave it there. She pushed it right up against the tree-trunk, hoping to be able to retrieve it later. Then shielding her face, she set off into the rain.

As she walked her mind ran back over the afternoon's visits. Constantly she had encountered either hostility or a kind of lewd chivalry of which only the French were capable. The men made it clear that they were not happy to discuss dangerous business with a woman, and even the women seemed unwilling to trust her. As she drew closer to each place she had become more apprehensive about her reception. And now her mind travelled forward to the reception she could expect tonight at Gouloncourt. She knew she must find somewhere to spend the night, but did not want to upset Claudine further.

By this time she was drenched to her underwear and shivering, and the rain continued to fall on her. Her limbs carried her on automatically, and as she plodded she hugged herself, bent almost double.

By the time she reached Claudine's door she was in a completely confused state. When the shop-bell rang, Claudine felt relief that her unwanted tête-à-tête with Thérèse was being interrupted until she saw that the newcomer was Liz. As quickly as she could, she bundled Thérèse out of the shop to avoid any further complications.

Liz stumbled up the stairs and into Claudine's bedroom. Claudine followed, ready to be angry with her for returning so soon, and after curfew as well. However, once she saw her state in the bedroom light she was all concern. Liz was confused, soaking and exhausted; she wanted to explain why she had had to come, but found her teeth chattering. Claudine quickly wrapped her in a blanket and forced her to drink a glass of brandy.

Once Liz had finished the brandy, Claudine helped her to take off her wet clothes by the newly lit fire before wrapping her in another blanket. Then with a comforting fluffy towel, she began rhythmically to dry her hair. Once Liz had got some colour back in her cheeks and stopped shivering, Claudine poured brandy and lit a cigarette for them both – a treat since they were so heavily rationed for women by the Nazis.

Claudine took a deep drag on her cigarette. 'Wonderful! I deserve a little treat after having to listen to that jumped-up tart Thérèse. She kept popping back all day; she seems to think I'm the only person she can talk to.'

'Does she say anything useful?' enquired Liz.

'Yes, she's let slip something that might be useful,' Claudine said, taking a sip of brandy. 'Apparently

124

Krieger's younger brother is due to be sent to the Eastern Front. I suppose that means they're taking divisions from the Western Front to fight in Stalingrad . . . '

'I'll pass that on to Gregoire,' said Liz, trying to struggle to her feet, but Claudine pulled her back.

'Not tonight,' she said firmly. 'It's after curfew and you're in no fit state to go anywhere.'

Inside herself Liz knew this was true. She felt feverish and miserable, but was desperate not to be a burden to Claudine – after all, she had come all this way to help. Confusedly she began to explain this, but Claudine stopped her.

'You're my friend, of course you can stay.'

CHAPTER 5

It was a grey day in Baker Street. Faith and Cad were ploughing through reports from agents in the field – the same questions and the same lack of answers. Faith noticed that Cad had begun to look permanently drawn. When she first met him, he had had an air of treating the war as a kind of intellectual challenge and she had always been the one who had over-personalized. Now Cad too seemed incapable of distancing himself from the complicated situation in France.

'So,' said Cad, 'submarines are definite then.' He paused. 'If the U boats are in and out daily, they must be grouping to attack the Atlantic convoys,' he continued. They considered other possible reasons for the troop movements in the area but none sprang to mind, although it did seem that the Germans were not yet attempting an invasion.

'The only significant build-up of reinforcements is in Bragues,' he concluded.

No reports of similar activity spreading to other areas had yet come in.

Gil walked in looking irritable and complaining loudly about the War Office; he had been on the phone to them answering their questions for over an hour.

'Bloody pen-pushers!' swore Cad. He knew just what

it felt like, having spent the whole of the previous day in conference.

'Why the devil can't they send in their MI5 chaps?' said Gil.

'Colin's on the spot,' replied Cad.

'But, dammit – he's not a trained spy,' Gil complained.

'You think I didn't point that out?' The strain in Cad's voice told of the efforts he had made and Gil and Faith were both surprised by his tone; they began to realize that this was not a standard conference.

Gil ventured to ask what was going on. 'There's more to this than meets the eye,' he insisted.

'Yes,' said Cad, 'they finally condescended to tell me. Combined Ops are planning a major offensive centred on that area – part of Operation Osprey.'

'So that's it,' sighed Gil

'Not only are we expected to provide all the data, but they want our help on the ground for the actual raid. Our agents in the area will be at much greater risk.' His frustration was evident.

Faith went out to get some tea and returned with a tray of tea-things and the latest message; it had just been delivered by messenger from Lois Mountjoy at the receiving centre. She handed the message to Cad who looked at it intently.

'It might as well be in double Dutch!' he exploded.

Faith instinctively jumped to Lois' defence, saying that they were doing their best considering that the reception had been so bad lately. Cad had no patience with the long business of decoding the jumbled letters and handed the paper back to her.

'You're the wizard,' he told her as he stood up. 'It's so bloody! There they are risking their necks to get us the

127

information, and we have to contend with this. There must be an easier way.'

Faith bit back her anger, knowing she must not allow herself to become too involved; she knew too many of them out there now.

Liz parked her new cycle outside the grey stone church at Carpet-La-Fontaine. It was a week since she had collapsed at Claudine's, but she still felt more weak and tired than usual from the cycling. She walked through the dreary graveyard with its large granite tablets, the untended grass rippling in the breeze. After the warmth of the sun it was cool inside the high-ceilinged stone building, though the air was heavy with incense. Automatically Liz placed some small change in the saucer and then picked up a candle, lit it and put it reverently in place. The church was empty except for a man praying in one of the front pews, his head resting on his arms. Cautiously Liz approached him and knelt down in a near-by pew. She looked at him and was relieved to see that it was Colin, as she had anticipated.

But he was not praying – he was fast asleep.

Liz shook his arm,

'Mm? What?' He woke with a start.

'It's all right, it's only me,' whispered Liz, noticing how drawn and haggard he looked. In fact both of them were feeling the strain, she thought. She still had the tail end of the cold she had caught in the rain a week ago and they had both been living off their adrenalin for too long. He handed her a package to deliver to Gregoire.

'Don't leave it around,' he instructed.

She knew instantly that he was referring to Matty and her carelessness and all her worries about Matty came to the surface.

'Have you seen Aimée?' she asked.

'Yes,' he replied. 'She needs company.'

Liz took up the package carefully and turned to go. She wanted to ask Colin to look after Matty, but didn't think it was quite right to ask this of him. As she was leaving, her eye caught a statue of the Virgin and Child and her heart went out to their closeness. She left the church thinking about Vicky.

Cycling off down the road, she headed for Kit and the farm. Some way ahead she saw a newly erected German check-point where soldiers were scrutinizing the baggage and papers of passers-by. Conscious of the package she was carrying, Liz made a split-second decision and before any of the soldiers had seen her she turned into the woods, pulling her bike with her. Wryly she realized that this was the second machine she would have to abandon by the wayside. Determinedly she began the long detour through the woods, careful to avoid any exposure to the road though at one point this meant a difficult passage through an overgrown path. She also had to skirt several farms, wary of the occasional barking dog drawing attention to her presence.

By the time she arrived at the farmhouse it was dusk; she had begun shivering again and her legs felt heavy and tired. Kit rushed out into the yard to meet her, having expected her much earlier in the day. Inside the warm kitchen she gave up her precious package and Kit exchanged it for a hot bowl of soup. She wrapped her numbed fingers round it; then, embarrassed, she explained about the check-point and the detour.

'Where is your bike?' he asked. She looked doubtful and he quickly got the idea.

'Not another one gone! I'll have to send one of Maurice's men for it again. In the meantime, you'll have to stay the night.'

'But Claudine will worry if I'm not back.'

'Damn Claudine!' said Kit with feeling.

That evening Claudine and Krieger sat sipping brandy in her living room. Claudine was being as charming as she could manage, although her mind kept flitting to thoughts of where Liz might have got to; it was strangely foolhardy of her not to return before the curfew. She tried to think of something to fill the silence.

'How is Thérèse?' she found herself asking.

'Still trying to read those intellectual books you lent her,' he said with humour. 'She's not had the advantages of your education – Switzerland you said, didn't you?'

'Lausanne,' she confirmed.

'A woman of many talents,' he smiled.

Claudine turned the conversation away from herself. 'I gather you too speak several languages?'

'Only French and English fluently, though unlike you I did not learn them at university but in a prison camp during the last war.' Claudine looked at him, sensing he wanted to continue.

'I was captured by the British and imprisoned here in France. It gave me a first-class opportunity to perfect both languages – and I'm not a person to miss an opportunity.'

'I'm sure.' Claudine got up to refill their glasses.

'After the war I was able to put them to good use when I joined an export firm which involved a lot of travel. Little did I know that it would all lead to this posting, but the war takes many people in strange directions.'

Claudine's mind had jumped to thinking about Liz and her eyes opened wide with shock as Krieger, as if by telepathy, asked, 'Madame Sarasin is still staying with you, is she?'

'She should be back soon.' Seeing that he was about to mention the curfew she continued smoothly, 'Unless she's staying the night with the couple she went to see – teacher friends. She's hoping to get some part-time work.'

She looked at him, hoping for signs that he was going to leave, but he seemed pretty well ensconced with his drink, enjoying the cosmopolitan atmosphere of her home.

The next morning Liz sat at the kitchen table convincing herself that she felt better. Kit had been very kind last night about her illness, but his closeness had made her nervous. She thought it would be best all round not to spend any time with him unnecessarily; he was far too attractive.

He gave her a message to take to Aimée to transmit and since her bicycle had been picked up and brought to the farm, she could set off as soon as she liked. She decided she must look in at Claudine's on the way in order to explain what had happened.

The shop was empty of customers when she arrived and Claudine greeted her with relief and began to relate the story of her uncomfortable evening with the beady-eyed colonel. Suddenly the room began to whirl round Liz. She felt her legs slip from under her just before darkness descended, and came round to find herself being undressed and put to bed.

'I can't, I can't,' she muttered. 'I have to take an important message to Aimée for transmission.'

Firmly Claudine told her that the message would have to wait, but Liz became so agitated about its urgency that finally Claudine decided that she must go to Alainville and deliver it herself.

*

Claudine and Matty had heard about each other from Liz, but never actually met. As soon as they confronted each other in Matty's cramped, untidy room they realized just how different they were. Claudine as usual was immaculate and gave off an air of chic efficiency, despite the danger she had put herself in. Matty on the other hand sprawled on her unmade bed, her papers hastily gathered together and shoved under the pillow.

'Celeste sent me with a message; she's not well,' explained Claudine.

'How do I know that?' Matty countered.

'My dear girl, I'd hardly rush out here for my own amusement!'

Matty looked at her with resentment: as a radio operator she was forced to spend most of her time in her room, just killing time, or out pacing the streets – collecting bits of paper from the same old places, sitting in crummy cafés – then returning to code the information and tap out messages on the sodding machine.

'It's all right for you, making up to the Boches and their lady-friends – that would really turn my stomach.'

'Do you think it doesn't turn mine?' replied Claudine with spirit.

Matty hesitated to comment on Claudine's sleek appearance; instead, she became businesslike and took the message.

'I'll send it in my next sked.'

'Sked?' queried Claudine.

'Scheduled transmission,' explained Matty.

Claudine was proud to use the real jargon when she assured Liz later that her message had been delivered. She mentioned that she was less than impressed with

Aimée because of her disorder and general rudeness.

Then she added casually, 'She's Jewish, isn't she? I can usually tell. Don't get me wrong, I've nothing against them.'

Liz was surprised by this comment, which seemed out of character. She remembered all the races and types they had studied with at the Sorbonne – it had made no difference then.

As soon as Liz was well enough to get up, she cycled over to report to Kit. As he took her up to the attic he had an impersonal air about him and she sensed that he was going to relate something unpleasant. She began to build up her defences in preparation for the bad news. They sat down beside the little table, the French countryside stretching out peacefully beneath them through the window.

'Someone has to go back to England as a courier with important information and I have decided to send you.'

'*Me?*' she repeated incredulously.

'There's no one else,' he emphasized.

All manner of objections came to her lips, but she remembered her training and the importance of obeying orders. Still, she was not happy and sensed that there was something in the situation that was not quite right. Was she being sent back because she was a woman? This she resented more than anything else.

'I would have thought you'd be pleased – a chance to see your daughter,' he said persuasively.

Suddenly Liz felt better. She had imagined she would spend the whole time in England locked in Parkgrove Mansions, being debriefed; it was a relief to think that she might get some leave. Now she found herself trying to control the eagerness in her voice; she had not realized just how much she missed Vicky.

Later Colin arrived and they all sat round the room with large-scale detailed maps of the port laid out on the floor, going over the information they had for London.

'The port defences are being considerably reinforced, but there's one weak spot . . . Here,' Colin indicated a cross on the map, 'the foundations are a bit shaky.'

'Because of the sand?' enquired Liz.

'Yes. I'm recommending they concentrate the attack initially on that spot. The details are all there,' he answered.

Kit asked Liz if she could go and get them some coffee and in her absence discussed her with Colin. He was obviously doubtful about his decision and asked Colin to comment on Liz's efficiency as an agent.

'How did she strike you as a candidate?'

'Want me to be honest?' queried Colin.

'Wouldn't ask if I didn't,' Kit retorted.

'Frankly I didn't think she'd stay the course.' He hesitated. 'It was obvious that she had reservations – a woman with a small child! Hardly surprising, is it?'

'No,' Kit agreed in a quiet voice. He was still uncertain.

Evelyn sat by the phone at Northover Grange, hunting through her untidy desk for Faith Ashley's phone number. Since receiving the letter, she had been uncertain what to do and had not been helped by Vicky's constant questions as to when she would see Mummy and Daddy again. Now that the child was safely parcelled off with a neighbour for the afternoon, Evelyn thought she would take her chances. She knew from her own experience as an officer's wife that the Army didn't take kindly to interfering relatives. In particular, she was uncertain of the reaction of Liz's jumped-up outfit, whom she assumed to be Intelligence. Suddenly she felt her age; this war made her feel unable to cope.

Faith was surprised to hear Evelyn and her voice was sharp with anxiety as she asked whether Vicky was all right. Evelyn assured her that Vicky was fine, but that there was another problem. She had received a letter from Liz's husband and felt there were intolerable pressures being put on her. Laurence, bewildered by the lack of information in Liz's letters, had written to Evelyn asking for an explanation.

Faith patiently reiterated that she was unable to tell her any more than she had done already.

'Which is precisely nothing!' retorted Evelyn. She had been trained in Army discipline, but this situation was beyond her.

'Sorry,' apologized Faith, knowing that this must be unsatisfactory.

'Keep it from *me* if you must,' Evelyn went on, 'but surely Laurence has a right to know? There's something else I should tell you. He's being posted back to England soon, so you'll have to speak to him before too long.'

She replaced her receiver and sat back, relieved that she had made the effort to ring Faith. Now the problem was in other hands. She simply could not be expected to look after Vicky indefinitely, solve all Liz's domestic problems, calm her son-in-law and keep state secrets. Faith Ashley would have to shoulder some of the load. After all, she suspected Faith of being the one who had talked Liz into taking her present assignment. She sighed and straightened her back, then stood up and decided to pull herself together. She had to rearrange the room for that evening's Women's Institute meeting and make sure that tea would be prepared for Vicky on her return.

Meanwhile, in London, Faith went into her meeting with Cad, Gil and Victor in Cad's office. They were to discuss Liz's future and the manoeuvres going on at the Bragues port in Area 3. Cad began by checking that arrangements had been made for Liz's pick-up and debriefing.

'How soon will she be returning to France?' queried Victor.

Faith looked at Cad – she knew what was coming.

'She won't be,' he informed them.

'But I thought . . . ' stammered Gil.

'You mean not at all?' asked Victor, surprised.

Cad explained that Kit wanted to replace her and needed an explosives expert to lead the forthcoming action. It was no reflection on Liz's competence.

'Thank God someone's seen sense,' exploded Gil, all his prejudices against women coming to the fore. Victor jumped to her defence saying she was a first-class agent, but Cad cut in before the argument became more heated.

'I thought Nigel Piggot might be the right replacement. He's hot on explosives and he's over thirty-five – so he won't be picked up for forced labour.'

Victor accepted the recommendation, seeing the need for an agent with sabotage expertise, but queried whether it would not be better for Kit to work with both Liz and Nigel. He wondered if there was some personal rivalry or relationship causing Kit to want Liz to return home. After all, he had been on uninterrupted active service for a long time – he must be punch-drunk by now.

Cad was dismissive. 'If I didn't trust Kit's judgement,

I'd be bringing *him* back instead of Liz.'

'It's a damn waste,' said Victor, but it was Faith who convinced him that it would be better for Liz to return from France. She had confirmed that Liz's husband was to be posted back to England, and this was a good reason for giving her a break from active service and a chance to sort out her personal life in England.

Matty waited by the dead-letter drop – a large hollow tree in the woods near Gouloncourt – for Liz to arrive. She wished she had someone reliable to talk to as she was going mad thinking about what Gregoire had arranged for Liz. She had felt such a heel having to transmit Gregoire's message asking for a male replacement.

Her life seemed to have shrunk until now it only contained a series of messages and her radio. She even dreamed in Morse code. Without Liz, Matty anticipated, there would be no release; she would miss her terribly. Cyrano would be the only one left with whom she had any contact, and she still wasn't sure how much she trusted him although she could see his attractions.

Matty drummed herself up into a frenzy of misery and loneliness. All her resentments against Gregoire and everyone else who behaved like the 'officer class' – the sort who gave orders and expected them to be obeyed – boiled up in her. It was typical that they had planned to send Liz back without telling her she would not return. It was worse that the main reason seemed to be that Liz was a woman.

Matty was always ready to rebel if she saw an order as unreasonable and she would have liked to refuse to send the message. It was so unfair! If they could take this attitude towards Liz, the same thing could happen to anyone. Alone in the wood, she began to wonder how far she could trust the bosses in England with her life.

By the time Liz did arrive Matty looked extremely distressed but Liz hardly noticed – she was so wound up with thinking about being in England again. She could already imagine herself in London . . . she remembered countless arrivals at Paddington Station, the warm engine smells mixing with the grimy dampness of the London air. Now she thought of the crowds of khaki-clad men and women, as uniform as the pigeons in Trafalgar Square. She saw the Corner House where she and Laurence had often met for tea when they were courting, and recalled with painful exactitude the smell of freshly baked bread and the cakes dripping with cream and jam.

Matty interrupted her reverie. 'Remember the first time we met at that War Office place?'

Liz smiled. 'You'd laddered your stocking.'

'And you lent me some nail varnish – then ticked me off for being a blabbermouth!'

'It seems like such a long time ago,' said Liz, looking at Matty with affection and realizing how much their lives had become bound up together.

'Will you do something for me?' asked Matty hesitantly. 'Go and see my Mum?'

'I'd love to, if there's time. Depends how soon they send me back.'

Matty covered up quickly. 'Yes, yes of course – only if there's time. And could you give her this?' She handed Liz a small package.

'It's been nice knowing there's another woman around, even though we couldn't spend much time together,' Matty continued.

'You sound as if I'm going for ever,' Liz said lightly

and Matty could find nothing to say. Instead she gave her a bear-hug.

'See you soon,' Liz said, disentangling herself; she was due to be on her way. She turned and waved as she got on her bike – her mind already slipping back to London and what to expect after the latest bombing raids. Matty stood looking after her. Now she really was on her own.

That afternoon Claudine was entertaining Thérèse to tea in her sitting room. She liked to serve afternoon tea as an affectation, copying the fashionable Parisian cafés. As were her clothes, so were her meals – everything elegantly executed. Thérèse enjoyed the sophistication; she was beginning to feel that through her association with Heinz she was acquiring a certain style and was determined not to be intimidated by Claudine . . . or Claudine's sense of taste.

'More tea?' enquired Claudine.

'Thank you,' breathed the bubbly-headed Thérèse. 'Oh, it's so good to talk to another woman.'

Claudine politely responded, 'For me too.'

'You have your friend Celeste, and plenty of others. Most of my old friends . . . because of Heinz, they barely speak to me.'

Claudine was becoming used to Thérèse's blithe assumption that they shared a common view of the Occupation. She was beginning to feel that everything was tarnished by the need to lead a double life. Liz had drawn her into a network of falsehood. She had always prided herself on an upright aversion to lies, but now they had become a way of life.

Thérèse continued, 'If only they realized I am trying to *help*. I look at it like this, Claudine. If we keep the

Germans happy, they are less likely to mistreat our people.'

Claudine assured her, 'I agree with you. I always try to be civil to them.' She hoped Thérèse would change the subject.

'These maniacs who blow up trains and such – what do they achieve?'

'The death of other Frenchman half the time,' replied Claudine.

Thérèse was enjoying her heart-to-heart and went on to explain that Heinz had no desire to persecute the French; he disliked having to hand them over to the Gestapo. He thought the Gestapo were thugs; he depised them, he was an *upright* man.

This was too much for Claudine and she responded with tongue in cheek.

'Except when he's lying down,' she said and Thérèse gave a dirty laugh.

'You wouldn't believe his stamina! That's the other reason why I have taken up with Heinz. Believe me, I wouldn't sleep with him just for the clothes and things . . . ' she confided. 'Just between the two of us, he's quite something in bed.'

'Really?' was all Claudine could find to say, but it was enough encouragement for Thérèse.

'Really! He has such energy.'

Claudine could only agree. 'Yes, he has to work long hours.'

'When his work's going well, it is better than ever. Tonight he will be raring to go.'

'Why's that? Or perhaps I shouldn't ask?' suggested Claudine.

'He is about to make a big catch . . . ' Thérèse leaned forward eagerly, pleased to have something important to impart.

Claudine hurried towards Matty's apartment, too upset to think about concealing her errand. Breathless, she climbed the stairs and knocked on the door, but there was no reply. She knocked again as her panic mounted; Aimée must be there, she *must* be there! Eventually she gave up and turned to hurry back down the stairs, but as she descended she met Matty coming up.

'Oh, thank God!' she exclaimed, but Matty was not pleased to see her. Claudine should never have been told where her safe house was, thought Matty; the woman was putting her in even more danger than usual by dashing over in broad daylight. She was about to tell her this when Claudine began urgently explaining.

'Krieger knows about the pick-up tonight. His men will be waiting.'

'Sod! You sure?'

'Yes, his mistress told me. Do you know where Celeste is? I must warn her!'

'There won't be time,' said Matty. 'I'll have to contact London . . . emergency transmission.'

Cad put out his hand to answer the phone without any intimation that the call would be anything but routine. As soon as he heard Matty's message he sprang into action, picking up the internal phone.

'Get me the BBC liaison officer at once. What do you mean – not there? Hell! Then get me Bush House, and quick!' If he could get a message to the BBC French Service in time, he would be able to change the coded message the BBC were about to transmit via their 'Personal Messages' to Kit and Liz; it would be the cancel operation message: 'Aunt Maud will *not* be going on holiday'. He would have to postpone the pick-up.

As he waited for the connection, he put his hand over

the receiver and shouted into the outer office.

'Faith! Faith!' He held on, tapping his fingers impatiently until she came in, aware at a glance that it was an emergency.

'The Boches know about the pick-up. Matty can't contact the others.'

'Oh God!' said Faith. Imagining the worst possible disaster, she realized how deeply she cared for Liz. She thought of Evelyn and little Vicky safely asleep in Devon, of Laurence returning home impatient to see his wife and of herself having to inform them all . . .

Cad meanwhile was shouting into the phone. 'I'm trying to get Bush House,' he explained to Faith. 'We've got to stop the message giving the go-ahead for the pick-up.'

'It's going out in ten minutes.' Faith's voice broke.

He slammed the phone down. 'Faith, you get on to the airfield and cancel the plane. The French Service is not answering. I'm going there myself!'

Cad had never been driven so recklessly before. The FANY driver took his life-and-death instructions seriously and they broke every rule in the book. He kept looking at his watch – he might just make it in time. On arrival he jumped out of the car and pushed through BBC security, putting the fear of God into the elderly security man who tried to bar his way. He panted up the stairs and burst desperately into the studio just in time to hear the original message go out. By the time he had scribbled a note to the announcer to make the correction and explained who he was, it was the last minute of the programme. He just hoped Kit was still listening . . .

'The previous message is cancelled. Aunt Maud will *not* be going on holiday . . . ' The announcer's voice echoed through the airwaves to France.

*

Kit carefully opened up the floorboards in the farm-house kitchen and took out his wireless. Liz crouched on the floor beside him as they tuned into the BBC.

In the hay-loft of a farm nearby, Maurice, Armand and four others were also tuning into the programme. As they found the frequency, the messages were just beginning. All over France people were waiting to hear news from their loved ones abroad.

Half fearing and half hoping, Kit and Liz heard the message they had been waiting for: 'Aunt Maud *will* be going on holiday.'

Quickly Kit switched off the set and replaced it under the floorboards. Liz automatically put on her coat and picked up her small case before they set off together for the improvised airstrip.

Meanwhile Maurice's group had listened to the whole of the programme and suspected that Kit might have missed the final correction which had come, to their surprise, right at the end of the broadcast. Leaving the others, Maurice jumped on his battered motor-bike and set off to warn the English.

Kit walked out of the farm with Liz. 'Which way will you go?' he asked.

'Across the fields. I daren't risk the roads.'

'I'll come with you part of the way.'

She knew that was dangerous for him. 'No,' she whispered.

'I want to,' he replied. 'There's something I have to tell you before you leave. I haven't been strictly . . . '

The threatening growl of an approaching motor-bike made them both freeze; then Kit pulled Liz behind the cow-shed wall, silencing her with a gesture. They watched as the machine careered down the farmyard track to skid in through the gates. It was only when the rider came to a halt close to their hiding-place that they recognized Maurice. His relief at seeing them was tangible.

Heinz Krieger sat waiting by the improvised airstrip in his well-padded staff car. His stony features gleamed white in the moonlight like a chiselled Egyptian god. He was a patient man . . .

In his Baker Street office Cad grasped the incoming message with trepidation. He breathed out through his teeth and Faith could see from his face that all was well.

'Thank heaven! If Liz had been caught . . . any of them . . . '

Cad broke in. 'It would have been ironic just as she was being brought home. I think this calls for a celebration.' He pulled out a bottle of Scotch and a couple of tumblers from behind the *Who's Who* and Faith realized that this would be only an interlude before the onset of frenetic activity. She politely declined and stood by while he downed his Scotch.

'Now we organize another pick-up, post-haste. The powers that be are furious about the delay as it is,' he said.

Unbelieving, Faith exploded, 'Don't they ever think about the *people* involved!'

The next day Kit arranged to meet Maurice to confer over the rescheduled drop. There were to be no mistakes this time. The pick-up would be by Lysander the following night. They would keep the information between the two of them -- and of course Celeste -- until the last minute. Kit saw that Maurice was looking grim.

'I've found out who it was,' Maurice said. 'That fool Henri Fournier gossiping to his sister.'

'Why can't they keep their bloody mouths shut?

'I've dealt with him,' said Maurice shortly. The failures of his men affected him personally; his pride was hurt.

The next evening Kit and Liz were again crouched on the kitchen floor listening to the radio. Liz looked at Kit's intent face – they both felt nervously that this was an ill-omened exit. This time round they were careful to listen to the whole broadcast; when the message came and no cancellation, Liz still could not believe she was really going to leave him. France was Kit, and Kit was France.

'Kit, the other night you were going to tell me something . . .'

'Yes,' he said tentatively. 'I had intended to leave it to Cad, but Aimée is right. I should tell you myself.'

Instinctively she knew what he was about to say, and why.

'I've asked for you to be replaced,' he continued. 'It's best all round.' So that was why Matty had been be- having so oddly in the wood, Liz realized.

'I've done my job all right, haven't I?' she asked.

'You know damn well you have,' answered Kit.

'Then why?' she persisted.

'It's too dangerous for a woman out here.'

'I'm prepared to take the risk or I wouldn't have volun –'

Kit didn't let her finish. 'Well, I'm not prepared to let you do so any longer.'

'Don't I have any say in the matter?' she answered

furiously.

'No, I'm sorry. I've already lost my wife in this damn war and I'm not delivering you into the hands of the Gestapo. Because that's what it could mean.'

Liz knew that it was not just that she was a woman – after all, he was not replacing Aimée. She demanded to know why she was being singled out.

'Because you've got a child.'

'Surely that's my business?' she retorted.

'And because I don't want to spend my whole bloody time worrying about you! I told you it didn't do to get too close to people out here – that it makes one vulnerable. Well, you've made *me* vulnerable, and there's too much at stake for that.'

'It's because I'm Jack's sister, isn't it?' Liz replied indignantly.

'No, blast you!' He held her arms firmly. 'It's *not* because you're Jack's sister.'

They looked into each other's eyes; quivering, she saw something in his face which she had never before seen in any man. He pulled her to him fiercely and held her close, kissing her with passion and desire.

Later that evening Kit watched the Lysander with Liz inside it fly low into the distant night sky . . .

Claudine sat in her sitting room drained of energy. She would miss her friend, but it was a relief to know that Liz was safely on her way home. Feeling liberated, she kicked off her shoes in an uncharacteristic gesture.

Krieger knocked on the door, then entered before she could speak. She tried to regain her poise – putting on her shoes again, standing up and offering him a brandy.

'No, thank you,' he said. 'This is not a social call.' His face remained a stern mask.

146

Claudine attempted humour. 'Oh dear, I hope I haven't contravened any regulations!'

'I have a proposition to put to you,' he said menacingly. 'This setting suits you and you are a woman who needs comfort. I don't think a prison cell is the place for you.'

'What are you talking about?'

'I have discovered who warned the British the other evening. Thérèse told you of our plan to intercept the plane from England.'

'Nonsense,' Claudine said in her most convincing tone.

'She admitted it after a little persuasion, and you were seen leaving here in a hurry after she had gone.'

Claudine gamely tried to continue denying his accusations, but Krieger forcefully leant over her and said in a hard voice, 'Shall we stop playing games, Claudine?'

She knew this was no bluff and felt helpless before him. No one had trained her how to deal with this.

'Either you agree to work for me as a double agent, or I hand you over to the Gestapo . . .'

CHAPTER 6

Liz walked up the street in her newly-ironed FANY uniform feeling totally displaced. Back in London, she felt curiously French. At such an early hour of the morning, only soldiers and the odd road-sweeper seemed to be around, drab and English in their regulation wartime gear. She had decided to walk over to the office at Parkgrove Mansions, though it was some little distance away. She needed to clear her head, come down to earth and readjust to the fact that she was back in England.

As she walked she seemed to miss a step as if she had lost her balance, and had to jerk herself awake. Turning round, she realized it was because an old familiar building on the corner of a well-remembered street had gone, and in its place lay bits of charred wood and piles of rubble. Although the gap was totally new to her, it was obviously not the result of a recent bomb, as straggly weeds had begun to cover up the damage. She had been away for longer than she had thought.

Liz walked on anticipating more changes, alerted by the faint glow of last night's bombing by German planes. She turned down a side road, hoping it would be a short cut as she did not want to be late for her meeting with Faith. An officious little man wearing an ARP helmet stopped her half-way down the street and told her to turn back.

'Don't you know that road's closed?' he said in a nasal voice. She looked at him, irritated, wanting to say that she had not known because she had been out of the country, in danger, doing her best to protect the lives of horrid little people like him. Stifling her comments she turned and walked back to her original route. As she rounded the corner, she was amused to see the warden looking after her with suspicion.

She was shown into the room Faith was currently using as her office, the bedroom in one of the top flats. She found Faith perched atop the dressing-table, her back against the gilt-edged mirror, her feet squarely set on the tapestry-covered stool.

Faith seemed nervous about talking in case she let anything slip; Liz found herself making casual conversation about what it was like to be back as she waited for Faith to come out with whatever it was she was holding back. It was unlike her to be shifty. Liz wondered whether she was overreacting because of the strain of having to be continually devious in France, but no – Faith obviously had something to tell her. Cad's arrival was a relief, breaking into the awkward silence.

'Congratulations! You've done a splendid job,' he greeted Liz.

'Is that why I'm being replaced?' she responded bitterly.

Cad was surprised – and perhaps relieved that she had already been told about this, presumably by Gregoire. It occurred to her that this must be the reason for Faith's evasiveness – not knowing how much Liz already knew. Nevertheless, the atmosphere remained strangely tense.

The reference to Gregoire threw Liz back to that

moment before she left France and she remembered the urgency of his whole being as he had stared deep into her eyes. She felt a wave of weakness sweep over her, wanting desperately to be with him. What if, she thought, I had refused to get on the plane and just stayed there with Kit . . .

Faith interrupted her thoughts by saying, 'Have you heard the good news? Your husband's back in England.'

For a moment Liz felt suspended in space and waited until she could breathe again. Confusion seemed to have invaded her; she had seen Kit so clearly only moments before, and now Laurence's face swam before her.

'Where is he now?' she found herself asking automatically.

'On his way up from Devon. I notified them of your arrival and he'll go straight to your Knightsbridge flat,' Faith explained. 'The sooner we get over this debriefing, the sooner you can go and join him.'

Cad had spread out a tourist map, the Outfit's own map and a War Office plan of Area 3; in addition, he placed alongside them Cyrano's hand-drawn diagram of the port which Liz had brought back with her. There was a worried frown on his forehead as he tried to reconcile the information. It was clear to all of them that the discrepancy lay between the War Office's pet theory that the harbour was being used as a refitting station for submarines, and the theory put forward by Cyrano and Gregoire that the Germans were planning a major offensive, which was the cause of the increased fortifications, the build-up of hidden ammunition supplies and, most importantly, the major troop movements around Bragues.

'All this depends on Cyrano's observations,' said Cad, thinking aloud.

The doubt in his voice maddened Liz and she bit her lips to keep silent. She was furious that the information Cyrano had risked his life to gain was being treated with such caution.

Cad continued to assess the situation, asking Liz for her judgements.

'I think Cyrano is correct in saying that the Germans are building up to something larger than the War Office had predicted. I'm sure that his observations are sound. The activity is centred on the port area he has pinpointed,' she replied. Encouraged by Cad to continue, she went on, 'I think Gregoire is correct to look for weak points in the German operation. I would trust his analyis of possible entry points and act accordingly.'

Cad nodded his head.

It was the beginning of a long debriefing session and by the end of it Liz was sucked dry of all her thoughts on every aspect of existence in Area 3.

After the meeting Faith accompanied Liz out of the bedroom-cum-office and pulled Liz's wedding ring out of her pocket. It had been resoldered. Liz fingered it gingerly – the join hardly showed. She had forgotten the need to replace it; Laurence would have noticed at once. Thankful that someone had remembered, she turned gratefully to Faith, not noticing how worried the other woman looked.

Liz's taxi drew up outside the Knightsbridge mansion block and she got out and paid the driver. As she straightened up, she saw Laurence crossing over towards the corner shop and hesitated, watching his straight back disappear. She realized with embarrassment that if it had been Kit she would have rushed after him and flung her arms joyfully around his neck. Instead she remained glued to the spot. As Laurence returned with a paper under his arm, she waited, noticing how much he resembled the archetypal Englishman as viewed from abroad, all character bred out of his face and demeanour. His face lit up as he saw her.

'Liz!'

Almost before she knew it they were embracing, and she thought how silly her cold hesitation had been. It felt good to see him.

They had decided to have a celebration dinner – despite rationing, they felt they had put enough into the war effort to deserve it. It was also a chance to take off their uniforms and rediscover their old selves. Enthusiastically Liz made for the bathroom; she was excited at the prospect of being able to look her best and relax in the atmosphere of a glamorous restaurant. In France she had not been allowed to make the best of herself, to dress in order to turn other people's heads. Now she was going to forget Celeste and really pull out all the stops; she would be Liz at her most attractive.

She lay back in the warm bath, luxuriating in the bubbles as her limbs relaxed – released at last from the tension of the last few months. Gently she lifted one leg up in the air, copying the seductive movements of a film star. She felt as though she was suddenly gliding through life after the weight of caution and fear in France. As she floated on air she began to contemplate her wardrobe – which evening dress to wear? She discarded the red *crêpe de chine*; with so many layers and so much intricate needlework – it seemed far too frivolous for wartime austerity. A couple of others were rejected for similar reasons; then she considered her standard blue, but it was too closely linked to everyday life before the war for her to wear it now.

Suddenly she knew what she must wear – her black dress. She remembered choosing it with Jack in Paris, when he had dared her to try it on despite its risqué scooped neckline, and had insisted she bought it. She knew it flattered her and made her look younger, though she had rarely worn it because it also made her feel uncomfortably exposed.

As Laurence handed her out of the taxi she felt a surge of excitement that they were 'out on the town'. Laurence was looking immensely handsome in his newly-pressed dress uniform and inside the restaurant she felt proud to be escorted by such a handsome officer. As he pulled out the chair for her to sit down she felt a closeness to him which she enjoyed; he must have shared this, for even in this public place he leaned down and kissed her.

Over dinner they carefully avoided any mention of the war and discussed the joyous days of their engagement at Oxford. They praised the quality of the food – Travussini's had never let them down. Later they toasted each other in ice-cold champagne.

Laurence raised his glass. 'To us,' he said.

'To us,' Liz repeated, smiling as they sipped the bubbly liquid.

'So you're on standby?' Laurence put down his glass.

'For a couple of days. Then I'm due for some leave.'

'We'll go down to Devon,' he decided. 'Headmistress said it was all right for Vicky to come home for a few days . . . ' He hesitated. 'I still don't understand what made you leave her and join up.'

'I tried to explain in my letters,' she muttered, wishing he would not bring this up in the middle of their celebration.

'You said you were bored with jam-making.' He sounded amused.

'I was!' She assured him.

'That can't have been the only reason?'

She tried to explain. 'I wanted to do something more. It's the same as the way you feel about sitting behind a desk.' At least, she thought, he would understand that.

'It's different for a woman.' He made no attempt to understand.

'No, it isn't,' Liz insisted.

'Especially when she has a child to consider.'

'I did consider her.'

'I wish we could have discussed it.'

She tried again in a calm voice. 'I know you're not happy about my sending her away to school, but . . . '

'Frankly, I'm *not*,' he cut in.

'There was no alternative,' she responded sharply.

'Of course there was,' he argued.

'Mother's busy with . . . '

'You could get work locally.'

'Anyway, she seems to have settled down.' Liz concluded, refusing to argue further.

'That's not the point. She's only five, Liz.' He would not give up.

'Jack and I were not much older when we were sent to boarding-school.'

'Yes, and you always said you didn't want that for Vicky.'

He was cross-examining her, she thought – as if this was one of his briefs. She began to feel angry and less tolerant – she had made her decision, done the work and now she needed comfort. It was too late for his arguments. But he was still waiting for a reply.

'I didn't know then that there'd be a war, or that I'd . . . ' She broke off, unable to explain what she had actually been doing.

'You'd what?' he encouraged, the barrister in him coming to the fore. She couldn't compete with his skill, not when she was unable to mention 'the Outfit' or France.

'Oh, need we talk about it now? This was meant to be a celebration,' she pleaded, hoping that he would just give up.

'Let's dance,' he said, relenting. He got up and held out his hand.

That night in their bedroom Laurence began to unhook her dress, kissing her gently. Liz felt a shudder of distaste run through her body as her black dress fell to the floor. Lovingly he stroked and caressed her, but she could only feel a blankness and it came to her that she did not want him at all, that making love would be an ordeal. He continued to kiss and love her, pulling her gently towards the bed. She realized with horror that all her earlier preparations had led to this moment of revulsion and she felt like a whore.

She pushed this to the back of her mind, trying to convince herself that it was the pressure she had been under in France which was doing this to her. She must not feel like this – he was her husband. As he slid on to her she began to act the part and slowly, despite herself, she responded to the pressure of his warm, sweaty body . . .

The next morning, as she had promised, she set off to the East End to see Matty's mother. She had never been to this part of London before and was disconcerted by the dilapidated appearance of the buildings and the grimy

155

state of the children playing hopscotch in the rubble. Even in the bright light of day she felt uncomfortable. As she approached the doorway, a squat elderly man came out of the front door carrying a garden fork. He looked at her suspiciously.

'You from the Welfare?'

'No,' she answered, 'I'm looking for Mrs Firman. I'm a friend of her daughter's,' she added.

He looked at her oddly and gestured. 'Indoors,' he said. As she went in he muttered after her, 'She's not a hundred per cent . . . ' and followed her inside.

Liz had prepared herself for a distressing meeting and was surprised when Aimée appeared to be a gentle, if slightly vague, French woman. When Albert introduced her as a friend of Matty's Aimée suddenly seemed to light up and was delighted when Liz spoke in French. She wanted to know all about Matty and even got up to make them both a cup of tea. Liz could see from Albert's expression that this cheerfulness was unusual. After she had drunk her tea, Liz took Matty's present out of her bag and Aimée unwrapped it with the innocent enthusiasm of a child. But once she saw that it was a bottle of Chanel perfume, she covered her face with her hands, moaned and rocked to and fro with distress. Liz stood there helpless.

'What is it, old girl?' Albert asked.

'She is in France . . . ' Aimée intoned, 'and they will kill her . . . '

Albert looked at Liz with dislike. 'You've bloody done it now, you and your bloody people! Now clear off out of it.'

Kit had called Cyrano and Aimée together in his attic

156

room at the farm to meet Nigel – 'Alain', the new courier. Matty was still distressed about Liz's departure but was determined to cover this up. She was not impressed with Alain whom she considered a feeble-looking type with glasses and definitely not for her. When Gregoire began by solemnly warning them not to expect to see much of each other, Matty hardly cared.

Gregoire went over his intention to monitor the new offensive planned by the Boches, also explaining that Alain was a sabotage expert and was to have special liaison with Maurice's troop. Cyrano was to cover for him as courier when necessary. Curious, Alain asked about the agent he was replacing. Gregoire brusquely informed him that all he needed to know was that her main contact had been Claudine de Valois, who remained a strategic informant.

Matty forced back thoughts of Liz and tuned back to the conversation in time to catch Cyrano and Alain making irrelevant comments about the unavailability of baths. She had lived in France for years without this bothering her – and indeed plumbing wasn't too sweet in the East End!

Though Krieger was with her, Claudine had never felt so alone. Suddenly it was as though she had no allies, no friends and was fighting a losing battle. She had no experience and no training to fall back on. Her house was in disarray and now she was facing Krieger. With an effort she controlled herself as he spoke.

'These British agents are not your countrymen – neither does their presence here cause the French people anything but trouble.'

Claudine looked at him, her head throbbing, desperately wanting to escape to a darkened, quiet room.

'And I am merely doing what their superiors would do in the same position. You think the British don't have their double agents too? That they don't resort to threats and torture? This is the dark side of the war.'

'I don't see what use I can be to you,' Claudine said feebly.

'You've been useful enough to them,' he retorted unpleasantly.

'I only passed on the odd item of information,' she said in a cowardly manner.

However, Krieger was well aware what her role had been and now he had simply to manipulate her into playing his game. He began by suggesting that she should continue to pass information to the British, only it would be false material supplied by the Germans. She wanted to refuse, but he conjured up before her the idea of Celeste being investigated. She vehemently denied that Celeste had anything to do with it, asserting that she was simply an old friend from Rossan and silently praying that Liz would never return. He listened impassively and then informed her that there was a possibility that he could shield both Celeste and her, but only if she worked for him as a double agent. Unhappily she insisted that she had no information, she knew nothing.

'I want the wireless operator; he's the one I'm after. I've had detector vans out in force and they know there's someone transmitting in the area, but the bastard keeps giving us the slip. You know where he is . . .'

Matty's face rose up before Claudine. Then she saw herself and Liz together as school-girls bright with the eagerness of youth. She saw Liz shivering and shaking with cold, grateful for the blanket and the brandy. Liz was very dear to her and if someone *had* to go, concluded Claudine, the answer seemed obvious.

'It's not a "he", it's a "she",' she said.

Once Krieger had got her to this stage, it was an easy matter to persuade her to talk. What he wanted was a full description of the operator and directions as to where he could find her. Claudine began to describe Matty and Krieger's mind jumped back to the little nurse who had bandaged his ankle. He felt anger that she had taken him in and slipped through his fingers once already. This time he was determined to get her.

Kit thought it would be wise to check up on Matty's state of mind; she had been left working on her own for some time and must be very lonely. He climbed the stairs to her apartment and to his horror found the door unlatched. When he pushed it open cautiously, he was even more horrified to see her code-book open on the bed. Where was she? At that moment she came rushing in and wordlessly he pointed at the book.

'Oh sod! I'm sorry,' she said without thinking. It was not an auspicious start.

Kit's other motive was to talk about Liz, which Matty was happy to do. At first she found nothing strange about his desire to reassess Liz's time in France. When she began to talk about the possibility of Liz being called back, he was still intent on remembering the past: Liz's various adventures with her cycles, her ability to liaise with all her colleagues and even to get on with the suspicious countrymen who were only reluctant workers for the Resistance. Matty found his attitude faintly disturbing. Then he suddenly remembered himself.

'For Christ's sake, don't leave your code-book out,'

he said again, insisting she reviewed her security procedures. 'You're getting lax!'

This was the bossy Gregoire Matty knew, and she was glad when he dropped back into character.

In Northover Grange the early evening rain drummed against the windows as Liz tucked Vicky up in bed. The child smelled of soap and baby freshness. Liz asked her if she had said her prayers.

'I've already said them. At school we always say them before we get into bed,' came the indigant reply. *Always*, thought Liz – always now meant without her. She bent down to kiss the top of Vicky's head and as she turned saw Laurence silhouetted in the doorway.

Outside the bedroom he took her arm, his voice concerned as he said, 'Isn't she a bit young to be at boarding-school? Perhaps we should reconsider our decision to send her there?'

Liz shook off his arm but he continued, 'I haven't asked what your job is, which I think is very restrained of me, but I think you should give it up and come back here to be a mother.'

Not wanting this to be an argument, Liz said flatly, 'I can't.'

She couldn't tell him what she had been doing, and why it was so important, so there seemed nothing to say. Her silence rankled. Unable to get through to her, suddenly Laurence was angry.

'I'm *telling* you to give up that job!'

The next day Laurence decided to talk to Evelyn. Was he being unreasonable? Evelyn did not know what to tell him. She understood his point of view – she had always felt a woman's first duty was to her husband and children. Laurence looked exactly like all the hundreds

160

of young men who had passed through her husband's regiment as subalterns. But the role of women was changing. There were land girls in the field and munition girls in the factories, quite apart from the thousands serving in the ATS, WAAF and WRNS. She had no rules to guide her and could not expect Liz to act like the Army wives of her own day.

Laurence began to explain his frustrations. He began by reiterating his fears about Vicky but soon switched to his real resentment – the fact that Liz was working and he didn't know what she was doing.

Again Evelyn completely understood his viewpoint, but firmly told him that she had no intention of interfering between husband and wife. He insisted on continuing the conversation and pressed her to acknowledge that Liz had changed. They agreed that she did seem somehow different, although they could not put a finger on it.

Finally Evelyn advised him that the only sensible thing to do was to talk it over with Liz. She knew that Laurence hesitated to do this, remembering from her own marriage to a similar man that there had been no open discussion of emotional problems. She hoped that a few days in the country would help both of them to put things into perspective. Damn this war, she thought.

The following afternoon they all went for a walk. They left the garden – now glowing with chrysanthemums – by the back gate and walked up the hill towards 'Three Acre Field'. Evelyn and Vicky walked on ahead hand-in-hand up the muddy path in their Wellington boots,

'Like Pooh and Piglet,' observed Laurence.

Liz felt distanced from him and from Vicky; she seemed only half alive. Life in England stretched out interminably before her, like the muddy path. Idly she

161

watched Vicky and Evelyn ahead, realizing how close they had become. She felt estranged from her own daughter, but knew that this was how it had to be if she was to play her role in the war. Even if she simply took an office job at the War Office, she would have to leave Vicky at boarding-school. If there were heartbreaking scenes at every parting with the child, she would be unable to bear it.

Suddenly Liz's attention was diverted by the shrill screams of an animal in pain. Ahead Vicky was pushing her way through the undergrowth towards the noise. The others joined her and found her white-faced and sobbing, staring in fascination at a rabbit caught in a gin-trap. She threw herself into her grandmother's arms.

'It's all right,' said Evelyn, but Liz knew it was not all right, that the rabbit's leg was broken. She was relieved to see Evelyn lead Vicky away.

'Wish I had a gun. I'd put it out of its misery,' said Laurence, standing motionless.

Liz looked at him in surprise. She had always relied on him to take the initiative, but now he was willing to let this animal suffer and do nothing. So she did what had to be done; she picked up a sharp stone and brought it down on the rabbit's head.

As Liz sat at her dressing-table that night brushing her hair, Laurence braved some difficult questions. He began by asking her whether she had handed over her French photographs in response to the radio appeal.

'Yes,' she answered, unsuspiciously.

'Is that when they recruited you? You are working for Intelligence, aren't you?'

Shocked, Liz realized she had underestimated him. She saw his face reflected in the glass, as hard and stern

162

as an interrogator, as she swivelled on the stool to face him.

'Surely you understand? I'm not allowed to talk about it,' she said appealingly, but his face did not change.

'Don't look at me as though this is a court of law!' she pleaded.

Sitting there as he began to demand a response, she remembered her mock interrogation. His harsh voice echoed in her mind and she felt as threatened as on that night. Automatically a cover story came into her head, and she used it persuasively, assuring him that she was working as a French translator. As she talked she began to wonder – as she had during that other interrogation – where the line was between reality and make-believe. She could see Laurence was losing his temper.

'What sort of translation course taught you to kill a rabbit like that?' he snapped.

'Darling, forget the rabbit,' she said in an effort to calm him down, but the muscles on his jaw tightened. She could tell that he did not believe her, but was unable to cope with the implications of calling his wife a liar to her face.

Blindly, he turned away from her; he would be too proud to ask her again and she guessed all the pain he was suffering. Knowing that she would not be sent back to Normandy, Liz decided that there could be no security risk if she told him that she had been posted there. In any case, he clearly suspected something of the sort.

She was not prepared for the fierce outburst of anger which greeted her revelations. He could not believe she had been irresponsible enough to volunteer to work as a secret agent in German-occupied territory.

'But don't you realize you could have been killed!'

'Yes,' she responded flatly. 'Christ, didn't you think of Vicky and me?' he accused.

She tried to explain. 'Of course I did. It was for Vicky I did it – and because of Jack.' But the moment he heard Jack's name he lost his temper completely.

'I might have known *he* would come into it!' he spluttered.

That was too much for Liz and she lost control. All this had been for Jack. All this had been to stop his death being meaningless, to stop his ghost from fading away. She felt that only *she* cared enough to keep alive the person that was Jack. She looked at Laurence with hatred, unable to explain. Unbidden, the image of Kit intent on his maps in his spartan attic room at the farmhouse, came into her mind. Confused, she threw herself into her husband's arms.

Cad and Faith sat in Cad's office talking to each other across a scale model of the Bragues docks which showed approach routes, fortifications and possible targets. Faith had a check-list in front of her concerning Area 3. She had overheard part of Cad's long and emotional conversation with de Gaulle and wanted to know what had been said.

'As usual, its the men on the ground squabbling over supplies,' he explained.

'Oh, Lord,' sighed Faith.

'There's been a dust-up in Area 5, with his lot and ours fighting over those food supplies we parachuted in,' he went on.

Faith thought he looked more alert and vigorous now that they were building up to some action in one of the areas.

They were expecting Liz to arrive for a meeting in a few minutes and remembering this, Faith thought it an opportune moment to mention to Cad a notion that had occurred to her.

'Our workload's increasing all the time and it can only get heavier as we send in more agents. We could do with another bod here at HQ.'

'Anyone in mind?' Cad asked, but as he spoke there was a knock on the door. Faith nodded significantly, but there was obviously no time for discussion.

Liz came in and sat down next to Faith. Cad asked her to confirm that the details of the model were correct. It took some time to check, and although most of the inaccuracies were trivial she thought she should mention them anyway. Faith took careful notes and Cad appeared impressed with her memory. It seemed to Liz an opportune moment to ask a question which had been worrying her.

'Does Gregoire know about this combined ops raid you're planning?'

Cad hesitated for a moment. 'He knows what it's political for him to know,' he said carefully, and she realized that this was the best answer she was likely to get. Obviously they were not going to make her party to more information than was strictly necessary. Faith reminded Cad hurriedly that he had an appointment and as he left he made a throwaway comment to her that her idea had been a good one.

Faith smiled at Liz once they were alone.

'Well, that seemed a successful meeting,' she said. 'Is there anything else you'd like to discuss?'

Liz raised the subject of Matty's grandfather, who had mentioned during Liz's visit that Matty's pay cheque was late again. The news did not surprise Faith – she was

165

getting used to his complaints – but Liz was not impressed by Faith's response.

'They really need the money,' she persisted.

'I'll chase it up,' replied Faith curtly and Liz felt stung into explaining how close she felt to Matty – the differences in their backgrounds had not mattered in France.

'We were all in the same boat. No one gave a damn if Matty came from Stepney or Kit's father had a title. We just . . .'

She broke off as she realized that she had given away the fact that she knew Kit's true identity. During the silence that followed, Faith wondered whether Victor's suspicions had been correct, that there had been an affair in France. However, when Liz explained that Kit had been a friend of her brother's at Oxford, this to her mind explained Kit's action and disposed of Victor's theory. Relieved, her faith in her agents was restored.

When Colin knocked on Matty's door she was deeply engrossed in coding messages ready for transmission. He didn't wait for a reply, but walked straight in – as usual she had not locked the door. As he wandered around looking at her new safe house, she found it quite distracting.

'Sit down,' she snapped. 'I can't concentrate when you're fidgeting!'

'I was just admiring your new palace, Madame,' he retorted, sweeping off an imaginary hat and bowing low. She could not help but laugh though the breather engendered by the comic relief was short-lived. She had to transmit to London and sent Colin over to the window to act as look-out while she set up her radio and began to send. She was so used to being completely exposed whenever she used the radio that it was a lovely feeling for once to have Colin's broad back between her and the world.

After a while Colin looked back at her anxiously, pointing at his watch. Matty saw his gesture but had to finish her message. She saw his face relax as she lifted off her earphones, transmission completed.

'Right. That's it,' she said.

'You were well over twenty minutes,' he put in worriedly.

'If they must give me such bloody complicated messages . . . ' she trailed off, running her fingers through her hair and making tendrils stand on end. Outside there was a screech of brakes as cars pulled up in the street below. Colin quickly turned back to look out of the window and then flung round to Matty, saying savagely, 'German's!'

There was no time to be frightened.

'Sod!' said Matty and for an age they seemed frozen. Then she hastily disentangled the aerial and replaced the radio in its case. From his vantage point at the window Colin kept her informed.

'Krieger's men . . . two cars and a detector van . . . Germans on their way up and Milice blocking the exit.' Their eyes locked in despair but she found her voice.

'Quick, hide the radio on top of the kitchen cabinet!'

Colin moved nimbly as beneath them they heard heavy footsteps coming nearer, loud voices and much banging on doors. Quickly she stuffed her code-book deep into her pillow-case. As she did so her mind ran through all the possible options. There was no back way out of the flat, so they could not make a run for it. As Colin replaced the pots around the radio case, she began to strip off her clothes.

'What the . . . ?' began Colin.

'It's our only chance, we'll have to bluff it out. Get your clothes off and get into bed!'

A German voice could be heard on the landing and the sound of splintering wood. As Colin hesitated a fist banged on their door and in a flash he was out of his trousers and into bed, crashing on top of her. Voices shouted warningly through the door and Colin called for them to wait a minute, but they didn't wait; they kicked the door in. Four men in uniform strode in and glared at the couple in bed, while Matty pulled up the sheet in false modesty and Colin asked belligerently what the devil was going on. The soldiers looked at Colin and Matty and reached the desired conclusion: the couple were too busy making love to have any knowledge of a wireless transmission. They muttered at each other in German and then left, slamming the shattered door behind them. The two lay still, listening to the boots making their way upstairs.

They waited in the same position, hearing the noises of the Germans searching the building. Gradually Matty stiffened under the weight of Colin's body.

'Move,' she hissed and he shifted, only just becoming aware that he was lying on top of her and how uncomfortable it must be. Now they faced a different discomfort – that of the mounting tension as they waited, hoping that the Germans would give up and leave. Cautiously they stretched out a few cramped limbs, until Matty was curled around him in relative comfort. The Germans were now checking on the roof.

For all kinds of admirable reasons of security, Colin and Matty had been controlling their desire for each other for a long time. Now that they had landed in this situation, the rules were irrelevant. Colin gently touched Matty's tempting breasts and she smiled. Gaining confidence he stroked her, then leaned over and kissed her lips. Tentatively she kissed him back. Her long dark hair spread on the pillow beside him as she ran her fingers along the side of his body. Colin began to explore her mouth and she responded, her tongue melting into his. Everything stopped – there was nothing but a slow need for each other, only the two of them merging and expanding to fill the void.

As their mouths became more urgent, their arms went round each other. They held on tightly, trying to get closer, realizing how much they wanted each other. Clinging together they rolled over and Matty looked up into his eyes. For a moment he looked down at her – caring, needing. Their caresses grew stronger and kissing, he entered her – their bodies slowly moving, calmly, carefully. All their desire and fear had accumulated, weighing heavy inside them. Now they prolonged each movement, gradually healing some of the damage.

Afterwards they sprawled on the bed, propped up by pillows, smoking a shared cigarette. Matty had never slept with anyone she really liked before and she felt closer to him than to any of her casual flings. They had been thrown together for so long that she had been forced to give herself a chance to get to know him, whereas normally she would have jumped into bed with someone she fancied at the first opportunity. This had been a new sensation for her.

They smiled at each other, not only liking what they saw but feeling a tremendous release of tension. For the first time in months they had shaken off the heavy burden of the German threat.

'I've never slept with anyone I liked before,' she admitted.

'I've never slept with anyone whose name I didn't

know before,' Colin countered.

'Well, since we're breaking rules tonight, mine's Matty.'

'Mine's Colin.'

'I prefer it to Cyrano.' They both laughed.

'You never did tell me about your love-life,' she continued.

'Actually, I've always rather gone for older women,' he confessed.

'Now he tells me!' she quipped.

Matty had never had the confidence to risk total trust in anyone. It was not only Colin who had penetrated this shield – it was the whole mission. The Outfit had taught her to be responsible for the lives of others as well as her own. Because of her determination to be in France and to help, she had forced herself to learn to become a vital part of a community. Circumstances were enabling her to reject the selfish part of her nature and to avoid following her mother into isolation and madness.

Very early the next morning Matty rose. Colin had left late the night before and she had to clear out to the next safe house before the police decided to recheck the building. She began to pack her clothes into a small suitcase; then remembering her notebook, she pulled it out of the pillow and placed it on top of her case. She had just climbed up on a kitchen chair and moved the pans from around her radio when the battered remnants of her door were flung open and Krieger stood there. She almost fell off the chair. There was nothing to say, and when he put up his hand for the radio she was clutching above her head, she handed it down to him. The game was up.

CHAPTER 7

The cell door slammed behind Matty with a thud. Her legs gave way beneath her and she sat down hard on a wooden pallet, pulling up the rough grey blanket around her shoulders. She huddled her naked body in the foetal position, wanting to draw herself into a ball.

Slowly she recovered. First there had been the shock of the arrest, then the humiliation of the car ride, the panic as she was forced into the cold room where they began to strip-search her. There were hands pulling off her clothes, crawling in her knickers. Rough fingers combed through her hair. Recalling the violation of having every orifice of her body searched, waves of nausea rose up through her.

The blanket felt rough against her skin and her legs were numb with cold. The only light in the cell was a single bulb, there were no windows and fungus grew on the walls. The peephole on the door revealed an eye. Having looked round and seen the limitations, she began to wonder what to do.

Now Matty thought back to her training and began consciously to call up the voices of all her instructors. They had prepared her by forcing her to go through a mock interrogation and she remembered the jostling emotions aroused by the experience. The real thing

would be far worse. It would be terrible, painful, *real* –
there would be no comparison. She shuddered; she had
almost allowed herself to feel conquered before they
started.

'Oh, sod!' she said aloud, the barrow-boy Matty
coming to the fore. That was the side of herself she must
hang on to.

There was no more time to think as the door opened
noisily. A grey-uniformed bully yanked her out and
pushed her, stumbling forward, down the cold stone
corridor. Her bare feet slipped on the polished stone
stairs but a hand pushed her between the shoulder-
blades every time she hesitated. She was determined not
to let the blanket slip. A final push sent her into the
middle of a room.

She was standing in Krieger's office. It was unchanged
since her last visit and Krieger smiled patiently as he had
done before, but now she was a prisoner, defenceless
under her blanket. She pulled herself upright; there was
no chance of her walking out of this one, but by God she
would try.

Krieger seemed amused by the expressions that
flashed across her face. He sat relaxed. Everything had
worked out for him and he seemed assured of being well
on his way to a successful round-up – a fisherman who
had felt the bite on his line. He rearranged the papers on
his desk, a sly expression on his face.

What was he waiting for? How much did he know?
Matty wondered. His voice was light as he began to run
over her cover story and it was clear that he didn't
believe a word of it. Fastidiously he pointed out the
errors in her papers, confirming that he had checked
various points in her story. Cynically he assured her that
there was no basis to her fictions and indeed they were
not very convincing.

She felt she needed to sit down, but that would be a sign of weakness. She set her chin, resolved not to let his behaviour weaken her. He seemed to have all the time in the world. He told her coldly that he knew she was a British agent, that there was a ring of them in the area and that she would give him their names. His certainty chilled her. He gave her no time to protest against his version of events as smoothly he continued.

'We have your radio set, notebook and codes. You might as well give us the transmission schedules.'

'No,' she answered defiantly, but inside she was far from feeling certain of anything. Trying to remember her training, she knew she must keep saying no, but she had gone blank on everything else. She thought of her mock interrogation. What had she said then? It had been easy – she had learnt a cover story and they had almost prompted her with the lines. She had no right story for this situation . . . and no prompter. She could think of no tactics. Matty thought desperately, she must work out a strategy, find a way through the maze.

'Face facts,' Krieger's voice cut into her thoughts. 'I have a radio expert standing by, so give me the information.'

She stood there silently. His voice had sharpened with eagerness because he wanted the information and she could feel the ambition that drove him onwards. She knew now that he intended to try and catch all the operators in Area 3 through her. Not knowing what to say, she said nothing. She knew that anything she might let slip could be a danger to the others.

His voice broke in: 'You have nothing to reproach yourself with; you have done your duty and Gregoire would be proud of you.'

Matty was unable to conceal her reaction to the name. As Krieger began questioning her about Gregoire's hide-out and identity, still she said nothing. She fought to hold down images of Gregoire that appeared in her mind; his distinctive red hair, his attic room at the farm, the letter-box near the farm. She must not see him too clearly – she felt Krieger might have a window into her mind.

'I don't know anyone called Gregoire,' she countered.

'Then he wasn't the man you were in bed with when my men searched your room yesterday?' was his amused query.

Now she was thinking of Cyrano – she mustn't put him in danger, she must keep silent. At least they didn't know that Gregoire was a red-head.

Krieger was waiting, so she bluffed, 'That was only someone I got chatting to in a café.'

He was unconvinced; it seemed such a ridiculous security risk, though he was only just beginning to realize how undisciplined Aimée could be.

'I was lonely,' she said, quickly forgetting her rules of silence.

'You'll long for loneliness once you're in the hands of the Gestapo!'

Matty shook inside with the strength of that threat, knowing there would be no mercy from them. Krieger looked at her coldly and told her he proposed to send for his radio expert with whom she must cooperate. Her statement that she would never do so fell on deaf ears. Krieger was certain that he had ways of making her talk. He called for the guards to return and take her down to the cells. She was being marched to the door when he asked off-handedly,

'Oh, by the way, have you any news of Celeste?'

Matty's triumph that Liz was out of it all, made her glibly turn her head and say, 'Yes I have! She's safe in England and won't be coming back.'

She was pulled out of the room before she had a

chance to see Krieger's satisfied expression and realize that she had walked straight into his trap.

Down in the basement Matty was dragged past her previous cell and looked at the guard in surprise. Roughly he told her that she was being moved. He stopped and unlocked another door and as she tumbled in she saw that this cell was already occupied by another woman: fat and middle-aged, with hair dyed blonde. She looked up at Matty, blowsy and sullen, and instantly Matty was suspicious. She remembered her training – this sort, they had been told, could be a plant.

Deciding to ignore the stranger, she sat down silently on her pallet. The woman spat full-throatedly as the guard left the cell and he turned on her.

'You will have no food tonight,' he said vindictively.

'I'd sooner eat my own vomit,' she raged.

He slammed the door behind him and after he had left the other woman turned over gingerly on her pallet, Matty could see the bloodstains on her back, which seemed to make her less likely to be a Boche spy.

'What's your name?' asked Matty.

'Marguerite,' she replied. 'And you?'

'Aimée.'

'That's right, keep to your cover story,' said Marguerite approvingly and Matty looked at her in surprise.

'The guards were full of it – you're the British agent they caught.'

Matty was not going to be fooled that easily and she asked Marguerite about herself. It seemed that Marguerite's place of work was part of an escape route for 'wanted' members of the Resistance – the brothel at Lasseron. Matty had heard that this had been raided and now Marguerite explained that the younger girls had been taken away and used 'professionally' by the Germans, but she was too old for that. Gouloncourt was only a half-way house and she was being sent on to the

Gestapo prison in Bragues – or maybe they would just shoot her, she added. Matty was instantly taken in.

'I wonder why they've put us together. Probably think it'll lower your morale, being in with an old slag like me,' Marguerite wondered aloud.

Matty was not going to let anyone accuse her of being a snob, she knew from experience the lengths to which poverty could drive women. She began to tell Marguerite something of her own story.

As a woman's scream echoed down the corridor, Matty's mind turned to her mother and she began to describe Aimée's condition to Marguerite: her nightmares, her fantasies and her withdrawal from the real world. Interested, Marguerite asked what Aimée dreamed about.

'Being buried under a heap of coal in the back of a truck,' Matty explained. 'We were here when they first invaded – had quite a time getting back to England. She's never been the same since.'

'How could you leave her like that?' pressed Marguerite.

'I don't know,' said Matty, 'but it seemed easy enough at the time. She used to drive me round the bend. Oh, I felt guilty about leaving her and lumbering Grandad, but I couldn't wait to get away. But now . . . ever since I came back, I keep picturing her as she was . . . always smiling.'

It was one of those miraculous days in the English countryside when the colours seem newly washed and as bright as a jewelled miniature. As Liz sat lazily sipping her breakfast tea, everything about her seemed permeated with a sense of being home and being safe. The whole trauma of France was like a scene viewed down the wrong end of a telescope. She felt herself stiffen as Laurence joined her at the breakfast table. He had an aggrieved air about him and she hoped he would not begin where he had left off last night. She was pleasantly surprised when he began to apologize. He seemed to realize now that he had no business to stop her playing her part in the war. She looked at him gratefully, seeing the gentleness and kindness she remembered from happier times.

'I just want to understand why you had to go into Occupied France.' Aware that he wanted to understand, Liz knew in advance that he never would. 'What made you change into such a selfish bitch?'

He had shattered her hopes of reconciliation and wearily once more she tried to explain. One thing she felt might help him to understand was her feeling that she was linked to the French nation and the French people. This war, for the first time, had caused mass deaths amongst women and children. As a woman and a mother, she wanted to play her part in preventing further deaths. Unfortunately this argument fell flat, Laurence's response being to point out that as a woman and a mother her duty was at home and it would not help to add her to the statistics.

Liz sat back frustrated as Laurence waited for the next piece of evidence. The wrought-iron garden furniture sparkled white in the gleaming sunlight, the potted geraniums adding just the right touch of colour to the scene. Uninvolved, thought Liz. She knew the house had stood here for over a hundred years and would probably stand for another hundred. The land had seen many quarrelling couples and later opened to bury them. She belonged here, this was her land. She was

177

fighting for a cause her ancestors would have understood.

Laurence began again patiently, in barrister fashion.

'When I was in Cairo, I used to picture you. Here, safe and secure with your mother and Vicky. Hell – it's what I was fighting for.' There was real affection in his tone. 'I'll never understand why you did it.' Impatiently she stopped him from maundering on.

'You talk as if it were something to be ashamed of. If I was a man, you'd say what guts I had and . . .'

'But you're *not* a man,' Laurence cut in. 'You're my wife.'

Liz resented his possessive attitude. She did not consider she 'belonged' to anyone, but had been given her life to live for a purpose. She thought of Jack who had risked everything for a worthwhile cause. She would not have asked him to hesitate in doing what he thought was right – fulfilling his destiny. It would never have occurred to her to prevent him from being the person he was. Laurence seemed to think that each individual was given a life already limited by social expectations; she and Jack were not like that.

Still he pressed on. 'I don't see that it's your problem.'

'I'm not just a wife, I'm not just a mother – the Germans are occupying people's homes.' She looked wildly around. 'You can't imagine it. If they were here, they'd be in our own house. The Abwehr have taken over Claudine's home.' This was her last attempt at explaining, she thought.

'Yes, that must go against the grain,' he said sardonically.

'You never like my friends,' Liz accused.

'Not when they're stuck-up selfish bitches,' he retorted. 'She's one of the most self-obsessed people I've met.'

This was too much for Liz. Everything was being sullied and dirtied by Laurence's stupidity and she had to get away from him. Pushing back her chair from the table, she strode off towards the rose garden.

When Evelyn arrived in the rose garden carrying a flat basket and a pair of secateurs, she found Liz seated on a low wall holding in her hand the remains of a rose, while scattered around her were blood-red petals. She had systematically stripped the bush naked. Behind her was a pile of petal-less rose-heads.

Gently, Evelyn spoke to her. 'Help me cut some roses dear, and then we'll go back to the house.'

Liz held the basket while Evelyn cut the roses, unaware how much her mother knew. Evelyn looked so sane, so everyday. She was unsure how to begin a conversation; perhaps her mother would help.

'I'm moving back to London,' Liz said, wanting to explain the difference this would make to her life. It seemed impossible that she could not find the words to describe all she had been through.

'You'll be going back with Laurence then?' Evelyn asked.

'Yes, he begins his new job at the War Office on Monday.'

Even the words sounded dreary and the days stretched ahead of her interminably. What was the point of it all?

'No more visits to Scotland?' said her mother archly.

Liz had not realized how much her mother had guessed. Everyone seemed to be clustering around her and taking over her life.

'I'll visit Vicky whenever I can. You'll still take her for the holidays, won't you?' asked Liz.

'Yes, of course, you mustn't worry about Vicky. I think you should concentrate on your marriage. I'm not blind and I've noticed how things are with you and Laurence.'

She was very understanding and slowly, Liz responded.

'Recently I've discovered a whole side of myself I never knew existed. I'm not the same person I was when I married Laurence.'

While Evelyn tried to comfort her by pointing out the havoc the war was wreaking in everyone's life, pointing out that Liz was not alone in needing to rebuild her marriage, Liz was wondering whether there were any foundations left to build on. Everyone else was impatient with her new-found self and she was being asked to revert to a 'normality' which to her now seemed unreal.

Cad sat chain-smoking at his desk as Gil peered over at the model of Bragues from the other side. They were going over the final plans for the attack in Area 3. They had accepted amendments from the War Office as well as new revisions from the Outfit's intelligence reports. It was clear to them both that Gregoire's men would be stretched to their utmost to achieve all that was necessary. More volunteers had recently joined up, but even more were needed. The whole area was to be mobilized. They ran over the parts of the operation that their team would have to carry out – mostly relating to power-lines and cables.

'Kit's got the training session well under way. Only thing holding them up is lack of ammunition,' said Cad.

'That should be rectified soon,' commented Gil.

'Yes, I've a plane lined up for Wednesday.'

'You've really got them moving,' Gil said admiringly.

'Yes,' said Cad. 'Area 3's become top priority. I must arrange some extra skeds for Aimée; we'll be keeping her busier than ever now.'

In a small office in Gouloncourt town hall Krieger stood over his radio operator, Dr Luntz. The desk was littered with Matty's code-books and German guides to radio usage. Her battered case lay open beside them. Luntz put on the headphones and began to tune in the radio, searching for Matty's frequency, hoping that an acknowledgement from England would confirm that he had rightly interpreted the codes. Krieger waited poised like a hawk. Nimbly Luntz's fingers fiddled again with the dial as at last a response began to come through.

On the south coast Lois began to sense that something was wrong. Matty's touch appeared to have altered – was she ill, Lois wondered. The message was stilted and the rhythm seemed uncertain, which was all very odd. They had gone through so many skeds together that it was as if they were talking each evening. Like two old blind men perched on a bench outside a pub, they recognized each other's presence, anticipating every move although they could not see each other's expressions.

Lois stood before her supervisor and Colonel Cadogan, who had just arrived from London. Her worries about Aimée's transmission had been taken seriously at Baker Street and Cad wanted to hear in her own words what the problem seemed to be. She could prove nothing. It was mostly a feeling, but was nevertheless a very odd one. To her surprise Cad took her gut feelings seriously, knowing how important it would be if she was right. She had been continuing to receive messages from this possible 'stranger' for some time and now it had reached crisis point. Cad went over and over with her exactly what she had experienced, and exactly why she felt as she did. He had to be convinced before allowing a test. On the basis of what he had heard, he rang Faith and they concocted a plan.

Matty was dragged to an interrogation room, dressed in a prison smock. On a scrubbed table in front of her, Krieger placed a list of names and watched her reaction as she looked at them – the names of every operator in the area, including her friends.

'These names mean nothing to me,' she said defiantly.

'They recur constantly in the transmissions we have been receiving from London.'

Matty felt her heart miss a beat. Despite her refusal to answer questions, they had managed to transmit to London anyway! Krieger was right to look so triumphant.

He saw her weakness and pounced. 'You must help me, Aimée, or I will be forced to hand you over to the Gestapo.'

The very word Gestapo frightened her. He saw her face tighten, and was pleased. With enthusiasm, he continued explaining tortures that were standard to the Gestapo, from pulling out fingernails and breaking bones in the hand, to burning the soles of the feet.

Matty tried not to hear what he said, struggling to think of something else. What was the order of the bridges across the Thames? She had got as far as Chelsea when she suddenly realized that Krieger had stopped speaking, having seen that her thoughts were miles away. She looked up just as his clenched fist smashed into her face, then lay where she fell on the floor, pain dominating her consciousness. He commanded her to stand up, and as she struggled to her feet patiently he began again.

'The list,' he said. 'Some of those on it are only marginally involved. If you do not differentiate between the English agents and the local farmers, all will be brought in and tortured and their families will suffer.'

Matty had no idea what to do.

'Aimée, I warn you. I will not be able to protect you much longer from the Gestapo,' threatened Krieger.

'I didn't realize you were protecting me now,' she said bitterly.

'Just tell me where Gregoire is.'

She clenched her teeth, determined that she would never give him away, would never be directly responsible for a fellow agent's death. Krieger turned on his heel and from the doorway called loudly for his lieutenant. He left before the lieutenant entered with his riding-whip; for a second Matty thought how incongruous it looked to be carrying a riding-whip with a military uniform. Then she understood. The two burly guards moved from beside the door and came to hold her down on the table. Now she knew why it was scrubbed. The lieutenant pulled up her smock and as she heard the whip swish through the air, she felt the first of many searing lashes.

Every time she mercifully blacked out the lieutenant

waited for her to come round and asked again about Gregoire. She said nothing, she would not speak. Her body was drowned in pain and she knew that once she spoke she would reveal everything; she gritted her teeth against it. She felt another searing stroke of pain and was certain now that they meant to kill her. That was her last thought . . .

The test had been decided on. Had Matty's radio been taken over by the Germans or not? Cad and Faith deliberated. The test question was:

'Have you contacted Micheline as ordered?'

Lois had been briefed and was sending it at that moment. The answer would not be long in coming.

'With any luck the answer will be, "Who the hell's Micheline?"' said Cad.

Faith could not bear to contemplate any other outcome. All the hours and days of work could not be wasted. Then she thought of Matty's life, which could already be in the hands of the Gestapo. She had never felt very close to her, but had to admit that as a radio-operator she was one of the best.

The green phone on Cad's desk rang and he took down the message in his careful handwriting before reading it aloud to Faith: 'Can you send further details?'

Faith's face fell. 'Oh, no!'

It wouldn't be the first time an agent's asked for more gen,' he said, weighing the evidence. 'Goddamn it, why can't it be conclusive? We'd better run the same test tomorrow.'

Matty came round and saw Marguerite standing over

her. Her back was on fire and Marguerite was carefully trying to unstick her dress from the wounds. She tried to turn her head to see what was going on, but every movement caused splintered agony.

The door of the cell opened and Krieger stood there. Matty felt she couldn't move, but knew she must show her strength to him, so with a superhuman effort she sat up. Her whole body screamed with the effort.

'You will be interested to hear that another of your comrades has been arrested.' Krieger's tone was vindictive.

All the people it possibly could be flashed in front of Matty; she must brave whatever was coming.

'Who?' she heard herself ask.

'Micheline,' came the abrupt reply, and she felt a surge of relief. She had prepared herself for a shock, but now felt drunk with the unused adrenalin and impetuously let forth, 'Who the sod's Micheline?'

The next day Cad and Faith drank a triumphant cup of tea over the new decoded answer to the trick question.

'It's Matty's terminology all right,' said Faith.

'Yes,' agreed Cad. 'Sod's not a word that would come trippingly to the average German!'

Faith was glad to know that their plans could go ahead; the drop of ammunition would be made that night and there was no need to scrap the operation against the power-lines. She and Cad consulted on the message to be transmitted over the BBC French Service that night: when Gregoire heard it he would send forces to the drop site. This time the wording was to be: 'Jean-Paul is playing with his toy'.

*

That evening Krieger was entertaining Claudine to supper in her own requisitioned dining room. They sat at either end of the long table, served by impassive German soldiers. Claudine had received a formal invitation and had decided it would be politic to dress for the occasion. She wore a discreet evening dress but no jewellery. Krieger, as always, looked distinguished in his uniform. A portrait of Claudine's great-grandmother hung on the wall behind him.

Claudine saw herself reflected in the polished wooden table – some of Krieger's soldiers must have spent hours preparing it. Her face and her great-grandmother's seemed similarly set and uncomfortable.

Krieger appeared quite nervous and Claudine felt she would choke. She did not know why he had set up this strange confrontation. Over the first course he deliberately talked of general matters and she was taut with suspense as she waited for his next demand on her.

She did not have to wait long. After his men had served the main course, he remarked casually, 'You have heard what the English do to traitors?' She tried to remain impassive at the other end of the table as he continued, 'We have found several unexplained corpses recently – shot through the head.'

He saw with satisfaction that she looked sickened and gestured at the food, saying, 'You know I do not always eat like this. The meal is especially for you.' She picked up her cutlery and began to eat like an automaton.

In a gentlemanly manner he continued, 'We need your assistance again.' Seeing her about to refuse, he threatened her, saying, 'There is your friend Celeste to consider.'

'I've told you she knows nothing of all this,' countered Claudine hastily.

'That's not what Aimée told me,' he added as Claudine's colour drained. 'Oh yes, we did get something from her. We now know that Celeste is a British agent and we also know that she is back in England.'

Imperceptibly he shifted from the truth into a lie: 'But she will be returning shortly and her reception depends on you.'

Claudine sat frozen. She seemed to have no choice.

'What is it that you want from me?' she asked.

'I want you to deliver one of our messages to the dead-letter box. Also, you must collect all the messages that are there. They will not suspect you, because they know you are a sympathizer. I cannot afford to have my men seen near the letter box.'

Claudine felt herself being drawn more deeply into the mesh of intrigue and horror. She did not want to have anything to do with it, but could not control what was happening to her.

At that moment Krieger's lieutenant came in and handed him a slip of paper. Claudine saw Krieger smiling to himself and felt sick.

'This makes the dinner perfect,' he remarked. 'The British have been taken in by my radio-operator and they are sending ammunition supplies. It was confirmed earlier – one of those ludicrous messages on the BBC.'

Claudine had long since realized that she had no idea how to deal with this whole situation. All she could do was to pull herself together and behave superficially like the pre-war Claudine. Although forced into deception, she would at least act like a lady.

Matty moved as fast as she could along the corridor. She tried to keep pace with the guard so that he would have no reason to push her, touching her torn shoulders. As she fell gratefully into her cell Marguerite sat up looking concerned.

'How did it go?'

'Least I got a cup of tea out of him. And a fag. Here . . . ' Matty passed the precious stub over to her friend.

'I didn't say anything useful, and Krieger knew it too,' she went on.

Reflecting on that morning's interrogation, Matty felt that she had handled it well. It was satisfying to see Krieger baffled, though it puzzled her that he had known he could get at her through her mother's disturbed condition – how had he even known of her mother? She was certain he did not know her true identity. Had she referred to Aimée in front of him? Could she have done so under pressure without knowing? No, she had only spoken of her mother to one person – not to him, but to Marguerite. She threw herself at Marguerite like an alley-cat, throttling her. Matty saw now that this squirming woman beneath her was a plant who had tricked her. All her rage went into her fingers and Marguerite began choking.

'You sodding cow!' Matty screamed, as she let go. Marguerite scuttled across the room holding her throat and retching.

'It's not the way you think,' she gasped.

'You're either working for them or you're not,' declared Matty simplistically.

'You know it's not as easy as that. They've got André, my son; he's only sixteen and they've threatened to send him to Germany.'

Matty's anger was directed at herself as well at Marguerite. She had been indiscreet and might have endangered other lives. Resolutely she turned her back on the woman, but the voice came pleading.

'I haven't told them anything important. You didn't tell me anything important.'

Matty realized that Marguerite was right to be frightened. All she had to do to get her own back on the woman was to squeal to any of the guards that she had discovered Marguerite's ploy. Then she would be no more use to them and this would mean instant disaster for Marguerite and her son.

'Please don't tell them you know.'

The model of Bragues sat immobile on Cad's desk. Neither Faith nor Cad was satisfied that the radio messages they were receiving actually came from Matty.

'We have to find out if Matty's been taken. At the moment we don't know who we're transmitting to, we don't know who we're sending ammunition to. You know as well as I do that Liz will have to go out there,' Cad insisted.

'You're sending her to her death. Krieger will recognize her and she won't have a chance. I still think you ought to send someone from Area 2,' Faith argued.

Cad firmly repeated the reasons for his decision to send Liz. Basically, he refused to lose Area 2 at the funeral of Area 3. If this raid was successful, it could be a turning point for the Allies and save thousands of lives.

'I'm talking about preventing a situation which could jeopardize our whole operation,' Cad ended forcefully.

'Don't individuals matter any more?' asked Faith.

'You're only thinking about Liz – what about Matty?' Cad countered.

At that moment Liz knocked and entered. Cad put his

request to her simply. She was to check on the ground as to what was happening in Area 3, since it seemed impossible to ascertain the facts from this distance.

Liz had been hoping that she could get back to France, but now that the moment had come she hesitated – it was a dangerous job. However, she felt the familiar thrill of action.

'When would I have to go?' she asked.

'Tomorrow night if I can wangle it.' He pointed to the drop site on the map and she took in all the location details. She was to arrive in Area 2 and, having made contact, travel on to Area 3.

'You've got to make contact with Gregoire . . . assuming he's not dead or in prison,' instructed Cad.

Liz knew she must remain impassive, that she could not allow her emotions to rise to the surface. Kit could not be dead. Fate could not be cruel enough to take both Jack and Kit away from her. She didn't care about her own life, the most important thing was to get to Kit.

By the time she arrived home to Laurence, Liz had decided how to deal with him. She was honest, telling him that she was going back to France. This led to the familiar row about her responsibilities as a mother and wife.

'I have to go, I can't let the others down,' she cried.

'For Christ's sake, this isn't some bloody hockey-match. To hell with the others! From what you've said, they're probably all dead anyway,' he said.

She closed her ears to his voice, refusing to listen to him any more. He would have to accept her decision.

'I'm not going to discuss it, it's my decision.'

Laurence began to complain that she must have been swayed by emotional blackmail. The plan to send her back seemed foolhardy and endangered her life. Still Liz remained adamant and suddenly Laurence was pleading with her not to go. He insisted that Vicky needed her, and when she seemed unswayed began to beg her not to leave him.

'You're throwing away everything we have. Don't I mean anything to you?' He was almost in tears and a wave of pity swept over her as she saw his face twisted with emotion. Her heart felt tugged by a spasm of pain. She had never seen her husband like this. Suddenly she could not bear seeing him look so pathetic. Her sympathy changed to disgust and she walked away.

In the East End the mood was just as miserable. Matty's mother, Aimée, was driving herself wild with grief – she had woken in the night screaming, imagining her daughter being tortured in prison. She began to beg Albert to go and save her daughter and could not get this image out of her mind even though he tried to calm her. He blamed the perfume Liz had brought and cursed her silently for stirring up trouble.

In the early-morning hours when Aimée's hysteria had finally dissolved into a fitful sleep, Albert was able to return to bed. He awoke for breakfast wondering whether the night's events had really happened, and lay thinking about his wayward granddaughter and hoping she had kept her head down. Secretly he was quite proud of the way she had insisted on going off to do this dangerous job. For a long time he had had a good idea of what her job entailed; she had always had spunk and could outsmart any of those toffee-nosed FANYs any day. She would certainly give the Huns a run for their money!

Thinking about the mug of hot tea he was planning to

make, he pulled on his longjohns and banged on Aimée's door to wake her up. The smell of gas caught in his nostrils when he was half-way down the stairs and he hurried, still not realizing the implications.

In the kitchen he saw Aimée's legs sprawled under the table, her head deep inside the gas-oven. He rushed over and pulled her out . . .

Matty woke, stiff on her pallet, as Marguerite whispered to her, 'I think I can get a message out for you.' She listened in silence, determined she would not be taken in again.

'I said I think I could get a message out for you.' Marguerite hissed again and now Matty was fully awake.

'Why should you do this for me?' she asked suspiciously.

'I know one of the cleaners,' came the low reply. 'Who do you want it to go to?'

'Someone called Claudine de Valois; she'll pass it on.' Matty couldn't see that she had anything left to lose. Since she didn't like Claudine much anyway, she might as well get her into trouble rather than anyone else.

Something must have alerted the guard outside, but his eye was applied to the peephole just too late to see their exchange.

Though she was on a hostile mission, the fields around Bessinville seemed friendly and familiar in the soft haze of the dawn.

As Liz climbed up the steep attic stairs she could not let herself believe that Kit would not be up there. Rounding the corner at the top, she saw a light under the door. She burst in and saw with joy and relief that he was there. The expression on his face was first one of pleasure, but it swiftly changed to horror.

'What in God's name are you doing back?'

They looked into each other's eyes. Explanations could wait. His strong arms engulfed her.

CHAPTER 8

Liz sat down on the attic camp-bed with Kit beside her, taking her hands into his and unwilling to let her go. She began to feel more like the person she wanted to be; it was a tremendous relief not to have Laurence there stifling her.

'Why did you come back?' asked Kit and Liz began to explain the confusion in Cad's office regarding Area 3. She drew a word picture of Cad and Faith staring dismally at the model of Bragues and Kit laughed despite himself. Then they came back to reality and she knew she must ask what had happened to Matty. Kit was matter-of-fact about it – they had just heard that Matty had been transferred to the Gestapo prison in Bragues.

Liz could hardly bear to think of her friend being manhandled by the Gestapo and tried to close her mind to any thoughts of what they might be doing. There was unconcealed anxiety on Kit's face as he watched her reaction.

'Don't think about her, there's nothing you can do. Let's hope she doesn't crack,' he said. Liz was certain that Matty was strong enough to stand up to the Germans; she trusted her friends – after all, hadn't Claudine come up trumps? Kit began to explain how vital Claudine now was to the operation.

The sun was up. Liz watched as the shadows began to

194

play over Kit's features, his bright blue eyes lighting up. She thought how precious this time was – a moment of togetherness before the dangers to come. Too soon, Kit was ready for action and Liz began to run through the alternative coded messages Cad had devised – enough to cover any possible analysis of Area 3's situation. Kit could inform them precisely about Matty's arrest and the present disposition of German forces. He could also estimate when Matty had ceased to be in control of the radio. This was vital – London needed to know exactly when the false messages had commenced, and what the Germans knew.

Kit would have to go immediately to Area 2, to send the relevant messages via their operator who could be trusted. He and Liz decided they must attempt to get a message through to Matty and to do so they would have to enlist Claudine's help. Liz set off for Gouloncourt across the fields, careful to keep out of sight of the roads. The only tricky part would be the last few yards through the streets. Overhead, as she walked, a flight of German bombers droned: on their way to London? wondered Liz.

Matty was drowning. The Gestapo man had his fingers wound in her hair as he held her head brutally down under the water. Her face felt as if it was bursting and her lungs thrummed with a fiery pain. She thought all the blood was going to explode out of her brain, but just as she blacked out her head was dragged up into the cold air which rushed into her grateful mouth. It was so good to breathe – but on that thought she was plunged down once more. Later, dripping wet and shivering, she faced the questioners again.

Matty had long since forgotten all the high-flown

ideals she had once had. She was not fighting for France, she was not fighting for the Allies; she had set her feet firmly on a bed-rock of resistance. She saw her father, weary and tired, dressed in soiled British khaki. Previously in this war she had tried not to think of him in danger but now such a thought was her only source of strength. He had been fighting with the Allies in Italy and she had no idea where he was now, but she tried to imagine that he was advancing in Area 3 and that to save him she must keep silent. She saw him cautiously treading a path through the cornfield outside Gouloncourt; everything in the vision was clearly defined, even the blue cornflowers and the red poppies by the farm gate. The lines on his face had gathered dark swathes of sweat and dust, the light reflected bright on his balding forehead. His brown eyes were wide and alert, but he had lost weight and had begun to grow a heavy beard. Again and again in her mind she imagined his face light up as he saw her waiting for him. She was not going to let go; she was not going to crack.

High in a church belfry, overlooking Cad's designated Area 2, Kit sat wearily on the dusty floorboards. Beside him hung the great bronze mass of a bell, between them a drop into oblivion. He turned round to look at the young radio operator whose set was perched beside another of the bells, the aerial emerging from the single stone window. As Kit moved, the boards sent up a fine cloud of dust.

'The artist is painting the house beside the bridge blue, although the swallows have left,' tapped in Jelu, the operator.

Knowing that in Baker Street they would now have to

discard all the false information received, Kit did not
envy them the job of reassessing their combined operation accordingly. He just hoped they would get it right.
As Jelu took down the aerial after finishing his transmission, Kit sat on feeling disinclined to move. Up there
in the belfry he felt far removed from the war. Idly he
looked up into the rafters and saw a swallow's nest – they
must have migrated by now. He would like to have
joined the swallows and abandoned Cad and his secret
war. Kit had been under pressure for far too long.

As Liz darted through the door of Claudine's book shop
the door tinkled and Claudine looked up, her face ludicrous in its amazement. Liz had expected to be greeted
with an embrace but instead Claudine seemed to draw
away; she stood up behind her desk coldly rooted to the
spot. Liz did not know how to break the silence – thrown
out of her stride by this unexpected reaction.

'What in the name of God are you doing back?'

Liz sighed; this seemed to be the standard reception.
Once again she found herself pleading with Claudine
that she had come to save lives.

'Yours has already been saved once and you have no
right to come back and endanger it,' Claudine shrilled
back at her.

Filled with consternation, Liz wondered how on earth
she was to deal with this hysterical woman. Claudine
came towards her and gripped her arm.

'Go back, go back now before it's too late!' she hissed.

'I can't, because of Matty,' Liz cried.

'Oh, damn Matty!' said Claudine, infuriated. 'I've
saved you and that's the main thing. Go back!'

Liz pulled away from Claudine's grip, puzzled and

unable to understand why Claudine was reacting this way. How could she feel she had saved Liz? What had the French woman actually done for her? As she asked herself the questions, the facts clicked into place and she knew the answer. She looked towards her good friend Claudine, with whom she had shared so much, and saw a traitor. Claudine's face changed as she saw the coldness in Liz's gaze.

'You betrayed her,' Liz said. 'It was *you!*'

Claudine could not find the words to reply; she opened her mouth silently, swallowed and blurted out, 'It was for you . . .'

'No!' Liz saw it clearly now. Claudine had not done it for her, she had acted for herself. All her life, Claudine had been safe and protected, cushioned by wealth and privilege, guarded by others, reliant on men to make her life easy. Laurence's judgement of Claudine had been correct, and it occurred to Liz that perhaps she had underestimated his shrewdness. She had trusted and believed in her friend; the pain of facing the reality was unbearable.

She turned on her heel and left the shop. Without seeing or hearing the world about her, she fled back to Kit. Afterwards she could not remember which route she had taken. Shaking, she arrived back at the farm to find Kit tipping refuse into the trough in the pig-pen.

'I found out how they got Matty. Claudine betrayed her!' she was stunned by the import of the words as she said them and reeled against the wall. Kit dropped the pail hastily and vaulted over the gate as she began to crumple to the ground. She came round in his arms as he carried her up to his bed in the attic. He put her down gently on the camp-bed and sat down beside her.

'Who else does Claudine know about?' he asked.

'Only me,' she whispered.

'Would she give you away?'

Liz could not answer. The Claudine she had loved would never have given her away, but this new person was a mystery.

'We must assume the worst – that she will betray your return to Krieger.'

His face was set and Liz knew that he had decided to take the necessary action. A traitor's mouth must be stopped for good; Liz knew the Resistance policy.

She imagined how it would be: the revolver shot, and Claudine's stained body. Could she let this happen? Then she thought again about Matty's fate and her resolve hardened – the important thing was to save her. At that moment a plan began to form in her mind as to how they could use Claudine to distract Krieger whilst they rescued Matty. This way, Liz thought they would allow Claudine to live.

As Matty stood facing the rough brick wall her body seemed a distant planet, coursing with pain. She closed her eyes knowing that she must not fall asleep or she would be beaten upright. She knew she had been there all night and long ago she had decided she could not go on. She was beyond any idea of beginning and end; she floated interminably, the wall merged into a river.

As she swayed the rubber truncheon crashed into her shoulders and she stood as erect as possible facing the brick wall. She must not close her eyes again.

She hardly noticed when she was dragged into a room where she stood between two guards. She felt like a ghost, suspended in space, her eyes burning in her cheeks. Two men sat behind the desk in the darkened part of the room and she waited for what was to come as the spotlight blinded her.

A voice asked again, 'Where is Gregoire?'

She remained silent and the questions flowed continuously, confusing her. The same voice kept repeating, 'We know you have met him, Aimée . . . Who is he . . . Where is he . . . Where did you meet him . . . ?'

Her head swirled and she saw her father walking through the mist; he smiled at her, pleased with her silence; he gave her the thumbs-up sign. Then a new voice disturbed her.

'Is it worth it? Tell us now, where is Gregoire?' The voice was familiar. It was someone she had met hundreds of years before. Who was it?

Earlier that day Krieger had been called into the office of the Area Commander, Major-General Stoscher, to be greeted with impatient discourtesy. They needed the name of the leader of the British cell. Operations were being held up by a stubborn fool of a girl and Stoscher was under pressure from his superiors to come up with the answer. If Krieger valued his life, he would get the information that day.

Krieger had to convince the Gestapo that Matty could be made to talk. He knew that he must sit in on the torture session, for he did not trust the Gestapo to pass on everything they got out of her. His face was impassive in the darkness.

He had one last threat; in his desperation as he drove towards the Gestapo prison, it had occurred to him that Matty looked faintly Jewish. It was worth a try.

The cultured voice continued and Matty realized it

was Krieger. He was accusing her of being a Jew.

She had dreaded this, but when it happened it meant nothing. She could not go any deeper into fear; she was already immersed in pain. She knew they would continue to do their worst because she was a British spy and she could not see that being a Jew made any difference. Jews were rounded up and taken to prison . . . that was no new threat.

Krieger had failed.

In the drawing room at Northover Grange, Laurence sat over a brandy. The weekend had been a success. He had taken Vicky to the local jumble sale and she had won a cake; the fact that it was made with carrot, and was eggless, hardly diminished her joy. The remains had been carefully stored in a tin in the kitchen, ready for tomorrow's tea.

Evelyn sipped her night-cap companionably, seated in a deep chintz-covered armchair. When she asked Laurence how his week had progressed, he began to describe some of his successes and failures, but soon his underlying worries came to the fore.

'What am I supposed to do while Liz is gallivanting about in France?'

'You're supposed to do what everyone else in the country is having to do – make the best of a bad job,' she said sensibly.

'Thank you, Evelyn,' he said with a fond laugh and they smiled at each other. Evelyn knew how ill he was making himself by worrying over Liz. It was not in his nature to take the sensible course and stop thinking about things over which he had no control. She felt sorry for him, knowing that her own husband would not have been able to cope in this situation either. She realized now how much strength she had needed to bear his frequent absences in the knowledge that he was often exposed to dangers.

Laurence began to explain that he could not stop himself from imagining all the various things that might be happening to Liz and Evelyn knew she must do something to help him. He needed to feel there was some action he could take.

'Ring this number in town and tell them who you are,' she said, giving him Faith's number. 'It's Liz's contact – maybe she can help.'

Cad was shown into a plush Whitehall office where there were no files or papers about and no maps. The only signs of the war were the sandbags outside the windows. Although the man who greeted him was a senior intelligence officer named Liddiard, he seemed to be more of a civil servant than a military man.

Cad knew that he had a difficult interview ahead of him and had to face up to one of the hardest decisions in his career. Liddiard knew about every aspect of the planned Allied attack and was the man to analyse the right course to take in Area 3, but Cad knew that the other man would agree with his own conclusions.

They began to discuss the Combined Operations' attack on the U-boat stations around the Bragues dock area which was intended to destroy the additional fortifications the Germans were building.

'We've been receiving false information for nine days, therefore the attack as proposed cannot now go ahead,' Cad began.

Liddiard pulled him up. 'What are you suggesting?'

Cad began to explain that his people on the ground could conceivably rescue the radio-operator, but this would reveal to the Germans that the British were aware that the recent messages were false. If, however, they continued transmitting as normal, they might be able to feed false information back to the Germans, which would allow them to mislead the enemy as to when the attack on the U-boat stations would take place.

Liddiard straightened his back. 'You're saying, then, that she's more valuable to us as a prisoner than out in the field?'

'Yes, God help us, that *is* what I'm saying.' Cad looked grave for he knew that once the deception was discovered Matty's life would be over. These were not flags he was moving around on a chart; these were individual lives.

Liddiard agreed and said he would summon a meeting the next day. As Cad got up to leave, he warmed slightly, shaking hands and hoping that Cad's wife was well. Politely, Cad asked after Liddiard's wife.

'She hasn't been too well . . . our younger boy was killed last month. A German submarine . . . his first time at sea.'

Cad could find nothing to say. Liddiard had tight control over his feelings and it was impossible to find words. As Cad opened the door Liddiard added, 'Killed by a U-boat; you could say I have an interest to declare!'

Faith stared up at him in disbelief. 'You can't *do* that.'

Cad knew exactly how she felt, but this had to be a decision based on strategy. He thought of Liddiard's boy, all that education and promise scrapped by a U-boat. The planned attack would wipe out this threat.

Faith no longer agreed with Cad, feeling it would be cold-blooded murder which she could not find it in her to condone. Intellectually she understood the decision, but this did not convince her that it was right. She had been partly responsible for selecting the agents, for their training, for their postings. She would not be responsible for murdering one of them.

Meanwhile the agents in the field were already planning the rescue attempt and though she found it distasteful in the extreme, Liz approached Claudine for help. The bell tinkled as usual when she went into the makeshift bookshop; she found Claudine in the back working on her accounts – elegant glasses perched on her nose and hair swept neatly up out of the way. She did not, reflected Liz, look like someone with a troubled conscience.

The French woman looked up enquiringly, her expression changing to one of guilty hostility when she saw that it was Liz. She sat frozen and Liz was just as uncertain of herself. Never in all their lives had circumstances pulled them so far apart. Their friendship had seemed invulnerable; now each had followed a path which seemed forced on them . . . and each had the power, perhaps even the duty, to condemn the other to death.

Liz hoped that she could get what she wanted relatively easily . . . without threats. All she needed was the name and whereabouts of the cleaner who had brought out Matty's message.

Claudine looked defensive, but Liz dug in her heels stubbornly and clearly did not intend to leave until she got her information. Claudine sighed, then seeing the contemptuous expression on Liz's face she was stung into a response. She saw that she would not be able to get rid of Liz until she had the name and quickly she decided to let her have it . . . whatever the consequences might be. Consequences were beyond her – she had lost the power to predict beyond tomorrow.

Once she had her information, Liz turned curtly and left the shop. Later she reported gravely to Kit that according to the cleaner, Matty had been taken to Gestapo headquarters in Bragues. The woman claimed never to have been inside the building, nor to know anything about the layout or be able to name anyone else who did.

Kit was disturbed by the news. Not only were the Gestapo more likely to get her to talk than Krieger and his men, but also it would be far more difficult to extract her from the well-fortified prison at Bragues than from Gouloncourt town hall. He realized that Maurice was sure to have a contact who knew the layout of the prison. Despite the fact that he was being hunted by the Germans, he felt it was safer for him than for Liz to go to the meeting at Maurice's farm. Her face was known; his, so far as he knew, was not.

Inside a pigsty crowded Gregoire, Cyrano, Maurice and Armand. Kit outlined the problem of rescuing Aimée from the prison in Bragues: he needed a contact who knew the prison layout and he needed to borrow transport. In reply Maurice produced a message he had just collected from an Area 2 letter-box. Kit was unbelieving as he read Cad's instruction that there was to be no attempt to rescue Aimée. The message was a simple

205

command with no explanation.

Maurice looked at him evenly. 'Evidently I cannot help you,' he said.

Kit had to make a quick decision, but it seemed obvious to him that Cad was not fully aware of the situation on the ground. Therefore he felt justified in reassessing the nature of Aimée's plight. He looked for confirmation to Cyrano, who nodded at him; then he looked back to Maurice.

'We shall go ahead with the rescue anyway.'

Maurice's face was set. So far as he was concerned, London made policy decisions and Cad was the boss. He was not prepared to risk his men unnecessarily. The four of them were caught in an impossible situation; their continued cooperation was essential, but they could not agree over this particular issue. Kit's mind ran over possible tactics while the others waited silently. As they stood there, huddled close in the sty, Cyrano found himself irrelevantly appreciating the subtle bouquet produced by the recently evacuated pigs, plus Maurice's noticeable penchant for garlic.

Quickly Kit worked out a way to force Maurice to support him. He pointed out that London did not know that Maurice and his group were Communists; once they were made aware of this, they would ensure that he and his men had no chance of getting their hands on weapons which could be of use after the war. Kit had recently received a consignment of weapons and ammunition which he was willing to trade for information on the prison layout and the loan of a truck.

Maurice considered the offer silently; eventually he gave a grudging nod. The atmosphere was such that they did not shake hands on the deal, but Kit was satisfied that the agreement would be kept, and he sent Cyrano off with Armand to locate the informant.

Later Cyrano, Alain and Liz sat at the large wooden kitchen table in the farmhouse, listening intently as Kit described the plan he had evolved to release Matty. Liz was impressed with the speed with which he had produced such a workable, if daring, scheme. He had absorbed all the information gleaned from Maurice's informant – a 'feeder' in the prison – and had weighed up the possible pitfalls; she felt they could rely on his judgement.

Hesitantly, Alain interrupted them: 'What was the message from London?'

'For some reason they don't wish us to go ahead,' Kit answered, 'but I've overruled them.'

Alain looked doubtful but Liz was impatient with his time-wasting. As far as she was concerned, the priority was obviously to rescue Matty. Alain did not seem to her to be suited to this type of work. He might be an expert with explosives, but lacked the initiative to be a natural secret agent.

Matty lay inert in the Gestapo cage. Big boots tramped by all the time and sometimes screaming people were dragged past. The place reeked of urine and excrement and the sweat of fear. Her head throbbed and she seemed to exist in a clouded blur. The one certainty was the pain that etched itself on her mind whenever she moved her hands.

She was lying on the damp floor and knew she must get away from the hard coldness but every moment was agony. Her hands were incapable of levering her up and she wondered what had been done to them. Slowly, she pushed her legs against the bars and shifted her body awkwardly, sliding herself into a corner.

'Pssst!' The sound seemed to come from above and

she turned her head slowly towards it.

She made out a metal shape on the floor beside her; a dish which was being moved nearer to her by a hand. The voice came again . . . she must try to listen.

'Stay awake tomorrow night.' Matty could not imagine what this meant; who it could be?

The words echoed through her mind again and again. She had been so bludgeoned and questioned that it was difficult for her mind to focus and she could not believe anything any more. They had tried to trick her so many times that she could not trust even the edge of a hope.

As dusk fell Liz slipped round the back of Claudine's home, not wanting to risk being seen waiting outside the front door. She tapped gently on the kitchen window and Sophie nervously peered out. As she saw Liz, she hesitated and put her finger to her lips, then moved away from the window. Liz prayed that she would open the back door.

A few seconds later, Sophie's plump figure appeared silhouetted in the doorway and she beckoned. Silently she pulled Liz into the house and led her past the sitting room and up to Claudine's bedroom. Once inside, she whispered that Krieger was downstairs in the sitting room with her mistress. Liz explained the urgency of her need to speak to Claudine and Sophie promised somehow that she would arrange for Claudine to come upstairs.

Time dragged by for Liz until she heard feet climbing the staircase. Claudine was horror-struck to see her calmly occupying the bedroom.

'Krieger is downstairs!' She stared at her friend. 'You must be mad coming here!'

Liz pulled her down to the bed, knowing she must not

let Claudine lose control; her beautiful face was rigid with panic.

'I've come to say goodbye, but I need one last favour – can you entertain Krieger tomorrow night? We have to know that he's out of the way.'

Claudine saw the earnestness with which Liz spoke. 'Are you really going?'

'Yes, this is really goodbye.'

They held each other close, unable to express their true feelings in words. Liz knew instinctively that Claudine would stand by her. For one last minute they embraced again, kissing each other warmly on both cheeks. Then they both crept downstairs, not even exchanging a final farewell before Liz left through the kitchen. Composing her features, Claudine opened the sitting-room door to rejoin Krieger.

Liz lay in the back of Maurice's truck, smothered by coal sacks. She was glad to feel the reassuring presence of Kit beside her. They knew that this rescue attempt was a gamble, but it just had to pay off. The cruel bumping stopped as the truck drew up in the darkness, then Colin shut off the engine and jumped lightly down from the cabin. Alain, Kit and Liz joined him under an archway, then Colin left them and sprinted across the open road to check that the coast was clear. When he gave the thumbs-up signal, they joined him. From their vantage point they could see the two walkways connecting the buildings comprising the Gestapo holding station, and could just make out that the upper walkway was enclosed. Though the lower walkway was open, a guard patrolled along it; with relief, they realized that he had obviously not heard the truck as he continued steadily pacing back and forth.

In single file they inched along the brick wall and entered the disused tunnel that ran beside the Gestapo station. So far, their information had been correct. They crept inside, Kit leading the way and using his pencil-torch to find the grille above their heads. Carefully he jemmied it open, while Colin held the beam steady. The sound of grating metal echoed loudly and Liz held her breath, expecting the guards to pounce at any second. She waited in the silence, stifling an urge to scream with fear and frustration. Kit pulled himself up through the hole and after a short interval he gestured down to them to follow.

Panting, they lay prone on the cement base directly beneath the walkway, hearing above them the even steps of the guard. When the steps had passed Kit signalled for them to follow him again as on hands and knees they crawled into the basement of the building.

Liz looked up and saw the dark column of a lift-shaft stretching upwards. When Kit gestured, she realized with horror that they would have to climb up it. Kit began to spreadeagle his way up the supports and with a silent prayer that the lift would not descend and pulverize them, Liz followed his example. The metal supports were cold to her touch and vibrating from the weight of the men above and below her. If the lift did come down to the basement there would be no escape. Eventually they emerged on the ground floor, where Colin stood guard at the bottom of a flight of metal stairs. While Kit ran up to reconnoitre the floor above, she and Alain waited, pressed against the wall. When the signal from Kit came, Colin gestured them on with his pistol.

Liz followed Alain up the stairs and Colin brought up the rear, looking behind them as he went. At the top, Kit nodded to the two men to ascend the next flight. Liz was left alone with Kit, who jammed the lift doors open to prevent anyone else being able to use it. Now they had to rely on Colin and Alain being able to locate Matty from the description they had been given by the 'feeder'.

Matty lay half-awake. She was almost certain that she was right to try and force herself not to sleep. In her confusion, she still half-believed that the Gestapo were tricking her again – trying to stop her sleeping so as to weaken her even more for tomorrow's interrogation. But no, she hoped against hope that the whisper had been from a friend.

Krieger turned to go. Claudine had kept an eye on the time and she knew that it was still too early. She had promised Liz; was it worth trying to keep the promise? What could she lose? Krieger bowed to her politely. It flashed through Claudine's mind that though Liz might not believe it, at least she knew how to keep a bargain.

She moved slightly on the sofa, deciding she would tell him how lonely she was – describe some of the needs of a woman in her position and how long it had been since she had known a real man. She would say how much she admired his handsome demeanour and capable brain; would sympathize with his responsible position in the Army and tell him how well he carried it all off. She would flatter him, and then drink in the consequences.

Alain and Colin crouched by a window. Its leaded glass opened without protest, showing them the roof of the

211

upper walkway a few yards below. Colin climbed out, held on to the window-ledge and dropped gently on to the walkway roof. Alain followed him but as they stood in the night air together, he shuddered back against the wall.

'What's the matter?' whispered Colin.

'No head for heights,' muttered Alain, embarrassed. Colin looked back at him impatiently – a fine time to exhibit phobias!

Gingerly they inched forward across the roof while below them they could hear the boots of the guards. Alain was fighting down his involuntary panic and Colin glanced back to check that he was following.

At the other end of the walkway, Colin pulled open the window and gestured to Alain to give him a leg up. He pushed the window open, then balanced on the ledge and pulled Alain up to join him. Together they dropped into the second building. Alain was relieved to get off the walkway and sighed thankfully. Colin orientated himself according to the information given by the 'feeder' and set his sights on the cage that should be Matty's.

Looking through the bars, he saw the crumpled heap that was Matty's body and could just make out her dark hair, encrusted with blood. He fought back his feelings for her; the main thing was to get her out.

They jemmied open the padlock and Colin carefully lifted her weakened body out of the cage. Carrying her, he followed Alain back to the window, cautiously checking for guards as he went. Alain led the way down to the walkway roof; then taking the initiative, he went ahead while Colin supported Matty behind him. He could see little of her face, but could feel how terribly light she had become. Alain hesitated, gesturing to the others to stop as he heard several guards come along the open lower walkway. Assuming they had passed, he beckoned the others on. Worried, he looked down; the sight made his head spin and he had to struggle to regain his balance – had to fight down his fear. Colin looked at Alain, but could not help him. He could only stand helplessly watching as Alain almost toppled over. There was nothing Colin could do; he still held Matty.

Alain's stumble had disturbed the gravel surface of the roof, some of which spilled noisily on to the walkway below.

'Run!' commanded Colin but Alain remained rooted to the spot, his fear overcoming him. Colin slung Matty over his shoulder and sprinted past Alain to the window. He threw Matty in and climbed up behind her, but as he scrambled up through the window he heard machine-gun fire and a scream as Alain's torn body tumbled over the roof.

Behind them an alarm started in the other building and they could hear gunfire echo through the night. Colin raced down the stairs with Matty over his shoulder. Kit and Liz saw them coming and unhesitatingly unwedged the lift door – all four climbed into the lift and Kit pressed for it to go down. In the basement he scrambled down through the grating first and Colin handed down Matty's half-conscious body before he and Liz climbed through.

There was no time to replace the grating. Their footsteps crashed noisily as they ran down the tunnel and behind them they could hear German voices calling. They emerged and dashed across the road, gunfire cracking around them as Colin revved up the engine. Two Gestapo men came running after them down the tunnel and Kit – sitting in the rear of the truck – fired several shots as it accelerated away. The first Gestapo man lurched sideways and fell, hit in the chest.

Liz watched as the Gestapo building receded and turned back to look at Matty. All three of them had fallen into the back of the truck and on to the coal-sacks. Matty had moaned, but now she was silent. Liz pulled her friend into her lap; she too was shocked to see how thin Matty had become.

Kit called to Colin tersely, 'Is Alain . . . ?'

'Dead.'

Faith sat on a bench in Regent's Park. Where there had once been a rose garden, now there were neatly-hoed rows of cabbages and carrots. Beside her Laurence shifted nervously; she felt for him and understood his predicament. Instinctively she liked his old-fashioned values and wanted to reassure him. Laurence understood enough about the Army to know that he must tread carefully; nevertheless, he had no doubt that any sane man would agree with him that a married woman with a young child had no business being sent into enemy territory. He wanted to be certain that Faith intended to have her replaced in the very near future.

Though she agreed with his reasoning and wanted to help, Faith could not allow herself to give him the true facts. She could not promise him exactly when Liz would return. Although she was expected within a few days, anything could go wrong. Much as she wanted to tell him that Liz's mission had been completed, even that was a risk.

Laurence wanted to go on to discuss his marriage. There was no one else to discuss it with, as he felt unable to reveal intimate details to his mother-in-law. He needed to understand the changes in his wife . . . wanted reassurance that these changes were simply due to her training. Faith wished she could help. She herself had been through an unhappy marriage and understood the pain he must be experiencing; but she knew that Liz was different, that having asserted her independence and a brave spirit, she was proving herself in a world which was far removed from her sheltered home in Devon. The only advice Faith could pass on to Laurence was to be strong and to be loving.

The truck bumped along a country lane and drew up inside a large barn where a light revealed to Liz the terrifying sight of Matty's hands. The tips were blackened and bloodied where her fingernails had been and the fingers of each hand were smashed and bloated, the hands grotesque, darkened like swollen and mouldering cauliflowers. Liz jumped down from the truck, walked out of the barn and gave in to a violent urge to vomit. Then she steadied herself against the farm gate, unable to think coherently, shaken by frustrated rage that Matty should have suffered so.

Inside the barn Colin sat in the back of the truck, cradling Matty in his arms. He was too shocked by her appearance to do anything but hold her silently. The effort they had all put into the rescue had given him no time to anticipate the state she might be in. He had no idea what to do; he could only sit there waiting for the plane to arrive to take her to London, to safety.

Kit followed Liz to the gate and put his arm round her as they stood under the starry sky. She was still shaken by their raid on the Gestapo station and the sight of Matty, but felt his strength as he stood with her. She turned and clung to him with her face muffled against his chest, hearing his heart's steady beat. Slowly she stopped shaking and eventually pulled away to stand beside him as they stayed looking at the night sky. She was about to leave while he had to remain, but in the silence they felt a moment of calmness and a sense of shared freedom. They experienced a closeness, a still unity.

The Lysander droned in the distance.

'Au revoir,' said Kit.

In Liddiard's office there was a strained atmosphere but Cad sat squarely facing the storm that he knew was coming.

Liddiard continued, 'It was irresponsibility of the grossest kind, resulting in the needless death of a British officer.'

'And saving the life of another,' retorted Cad. He was determined to stand up for his team and privately he cheered them on. He was still impressed by the performance of his agents. There would be a time to dress them down, but definitely not in front of the War Office. His makeshift Outfit continued to prove themselves.

In this very office they had sat and made their plans. They had discussed what needed to be done and agreed on a course of action.

'You knew what you had to do,' drummed in Liddiard. 'The rules apply to everybody.'

'I did authorize the message not to attempt a rescue,' responded Cad stolidly.

'Your Outfit doesn't understand the meaning of discipline. Orders, Cadogan, orders! Your people are amateurs,' he fumed.

'Yes, sir,' replied Cad evenly.

A noise woke Claudine before dawn and she sat up and switched on her bedside light. Hearing the sound of a yawn, she started as she realized that Krieger was in bed beside her, and turned to look at him. His fair hair was tousled and darkened with sweat. She remembered the events of the previous night, but quickly decided it would be pleasanter to forget.

Before either of them had a chance to speak they heard the sound of splintering wood, and voices, then boots stamping up the stairs. Three thuggish soldiers stood in the bedroom doorway and behind them she could hear Sophie's voice calling out in dismay. They pulled Claudine out of the bed and before she could turn to Krieger, she was bundled next door into the bathroom. A soldier picked up her discarded dress and told her to put it on. She had to force on her shoes without stockings; then she was dragged downstairs.

Outside they handcuffed her and pushed her into the back of an Abwehr staff car. Through the open door she could see Krieger being frogmarched out of the house; his face was bleeding and he was still protesting. Obviously he had been hurried into his uniform; he had neither jacket nor cap, his shirt was undone and hung outside his trousers. Major-General Stoscher stood beside the car glowering at Krieger and shaking his head. Claudine watched as Krieger's own men handcuffed him and drove him away in a black van.

*

Cad and Faith were celebrating. He prised the cork out of a bottle of champagne and deftly filled two glasses.

'A triumph, after all,' said Faith, raising her glass.

'A triumph for you, certainly,' agreed Cad and Faith's eyes shone with unshed tears. This was what it had all been about – the team spirit – the brave initiative to save Matty's life. She glowed.

Matty walked down the narrow Stepney Street, her gaze on Albert's terraced home. Walking slowly, her pace decreased as she neared the house. She had been told that her mother was dead, but now it was hard to know how to feel. She still half expected to see her mother sitting sewing at the kitchen table; it was impossible to imagine 'home' without Aimée. More than a lifetime seemed to have passed since last she had left. She herself had been through an experience that was beyond comprehension and shock still stared out of her eyes. Three weeks after her escape doctors had almost mended her body, but nobody could remove the scars from her mind.

She stood out in the street, unable to summon up the strength to go in. Voices floated from the open windows of the next-door house, but someone had pulled down the blinds at Albert's windows. It had become unreal, a stranger's home.

Then Albert opened the door. He came out on to the doorstep and saw her. Neither knew what to say but he saw her pale thin face, the white bandaged hands, her still loneliness.

He stepped out into the street, put his arm round her and guided her into the house.

*

Liz had come home. She walked through the house in her FANY uniform that sunny afternoon and found Laurence pushing Vicky higher and higher on her swing in the back garden. She saw her mother before Laurence did and sprang from the swing, almost causing him to topple over.

'Mummy!' she called as she sped across the lawn into Liz's arms. Liz looked down at her daughter's eager face and then glanced up at Laurence – he was still standing over by the swing. She could feel the tension between them which prevented him from coming over to greet her, so she took Vicky's hand and walked across the lawn to meet him. As he came to join her, she saw his anxious face softening into a smile. Husband and wife looked at each other over their excited daughter's head.

'Hello, Laurence,' Liz found herself saying.

'I've been so worried about you,' he managed to reply.

'There was no need,' Liz murmured.

Vicky held on to one arm of each of her parents tightly, as if afraid they might disappear, while they stood facing each other unsure how to proceed. Finally Laurence leaned towards Liz and gently kissed her cheek.

'Mummy, Daddy, come and push me in the swing!' Vicky impatiently tugged at their arms and the three of them made their way back to the oak tree where Liz and Laurence stood on either side of the swing, pushing the happy little girl back and forth.

Laurence smiled at his wife. 'I'm so pleased to have you back,' he said and kissed her again.

She knew he was trying to say the right thing, but she could not bring herself to respond reassuringly. In fact she could not feel anything inside. There was no love for her husband. She told herself it was shock – the mission,

Matty, danger, Kit. She had needed desperately to take some action – to do something significant for the war, her family, Jack . . . and somehow she had been sure this would bring her a sense of fulfilment. But there was nothing. It was futile to think she had achieved anything for Jack. Her beloved brother was dead – a fact she had not really allowed herself to believe before. An emptiness gaped inside her, mauled at her.

Laurence stopped pushing the swing and put an arm round her shoulders.

'I've got two weeks' leave due.' He waited for her response and then continued, 'We ought to go away together.'

She knew what he wanted; the old Liz. But she was no longer that person.

Laurence looked at Vicky and then back at Liz.

'Thank God it's all over and we can get back to normal . . .'

A Selection of Arrow Bestsellers

☐ Live Flesh	Ruth Rendell	£2.75
☐ Contact	Carl Sagan	£3.50
☐ Yeager	Chuck Yeager	£3.95
☐ The Lilac Bus	Maeve Binchy	£2.50
☐ 500 Mile Walkies	Mark Wallington	£2.50
☐ Staying Off the Beaten Track	Elizabeth Gundrey	£4.95
☐ A Better World Than This	Marie Joseph	£2.95
☐ No Enemy But Time	Evelyn Anthony	£2.95
☐ Rates of Exchange	Malcolm Bradbury	£3.50
☐ For My Brother's Sins	Sheelagh Kelly	£3.50
☐ Carrott Roots	Jasper Carrott	£3.50
☐ Colours Aloft	Alexander Kent	£2.95
☐ Blind Run	Brian Freemantle	£2.50
☐ The Stationmaster's Daughter	Pamela Oldfield	£2.95
☐ Speaker for the Dead	Orson Scott Card	£2.95
☐ Football is a Funny Game	Ian St John and Jimmy Greaves	£3.95
☐ Crowned in a Far Country	Princess Michael of Kent	£4.95

Prices and other details are liable to change

ARROW BOOKS, BOOKSERVICE BY POST, PO BOX 29, DOUGLAS, ISLE
OF MAN, BRITISH ISLES

NAME ....

ADDRESS ....

....

....

Please enclose a cheque or postal order made out to Arrow Books Ltd. for the amount
due and allow the following for postage and packing.

U.K. CUSTOMERS: Please allow 22p per book to a maximum of £3.00.

B.F.P.O. & EIRE: Please allow 22p per book to a maximum of £3.00.

OVERSEAS CUSTOMERS: Please allow 22p per book.

Whilst every effort is made to keep prices low it is sometimes necessary to increase cover
prices at short notice. Arrow Books reserve the right to show new retail prices on covers
which may differ from those previously advertised in the text or elsewhere.

Bestselling War Fiction and Non-Fiction

☐ Passage to Mutiny	Alexander Kent	£2.95
☐ The Flag Captain	Alexander Kent	£2.95
☐ Badge of Glory	Douglas Reeman	£2.95
☐ Winged Escort	Douglas Reeman	£2.95
☐ Army of Shadows	John Harris	£2.50
☐ Decoy	Dudley Pope	£2.95
☐ Curse of the Death's Head	Rupert Butler	£2.25
☐ Gestapo	Rupert Butler	£2.75
☐ Tumult in the Clouds	James A. Goodson	£3.50
☐ Sigh for a Merlin	Alex Henshaw	£2.95
☐ Morning Glory	Stephen Howarth	£4.95
☐ The Doodlebugs	Norman Longmate	£4.95
☐ Colditz – The Full Story	Major P. Reid	£2.95
☐ Johnny Gurkha	E.D. Smith	£2.95
☐ Typhoon Pilot	Desmond Scott	£2.95
☐ The Rommel Papers	B.H. Liddell Hart	£5.95
☐ Colours Aloft	Alexander Kent	£2.95

Prices and other details are liable to change

ARROW BOOKS, BOOKSERVICE BY POST, PO BOX 29, DOUGLAS, ISLE OF MAN, BRITISH ISLES

NAME ....

ADDRESS ....

....

....

Please enclose a cheque or postal order made out to Arrow Books Ltd. for the amount due and allow the following for postage and packing.

U.K. CUSTOMERS: Please allow 22p per book to a maximum of £3.00.

B.F.P.O. & EIRE: Please allow 22p per book to a maximum of £3.00.

OVERSEAS CUSTOMERS: Please allow 22p per book.

Whilst every effort is made to keep prices low it is sometimes necessary to increase cover prices at short notice. Arrow Books reserve the right to show new retail prices on covers which may differ from those previously advertised in the text or elsewhere.

Bestselling Fiction

☐ Hiroshima Joe	Martin Booth	£2.95
☐ Voices on the Wind	Evelyn Anthony	£2.50
☐ The Pianoplayers	Anthony Burgess	£2.50
☐ Prizzi's Honour	Richard Condon	£2.95
☐ Queen's Play	Dorothy Dunnett	£3.50
☐ Duncton Wood	William Horwood	£3.50
☐ In Gallant Company	Alexander Kent	£2.50
☐ The Fast Men	Tom McNab	£2.95
☐ A Ship With No Name	Christopher Nicole	£2.95
☐ Contact	Carl Sagan	£3.50
☐ Uncle Mort's North Country	Peter Tinniswood	£2.50
☐ Fletch	Gregory Mcdonald	£1.95
☐ A Better World Than This	Marie Joseph	£2.95
☐ The Lilac Bus	Maeve Binchy	£2.50
☐ The Gooding Girl	Pamela Oldfield	£2.95

Prices and other details are liable to change

ARROW BOOKS, BOOKSERVICE BY POST, PO BOX 29, DOUGLAS, ISLE OF MAN, BRITISH ISLES

NAME ....

ADDRESS ....

....

....

Please enclose a cheque or postal order made out to Arrow Books Ltd. for the amount due and allow the following for postage and packing.

U.K. CUSTOMERS: Please allow 22p per book to a maximum of £3.00.

B.F.P.O. & EIRE: Please allow 22p per book to a maximum of £3.00.

OVERSEAS CUSTOMERS: Please allow 22p per book.

Whilst every effort is made to keep prices low it is sometimes necessary to increase cover prices at short notice. Arrow Books reserve the right to show new retail prices on covers which may differ from those previously advertised in the text or elsewhere.

Bestselling Fiction

☐ Toll for the Brave	Jack Higgins	£2.25
☐ Basikasingo	John Matthews	£2.95
☐ Where No Man Cries	Emma Blair	£2.50
☐ Saudi	Laurie Devine	£2.95
☐ The Clogger's Child	Marie Joseph	£2.50
☐ The Gooding Girl	Pamela Oldfield	£2.95
☐ The Running Years	Claire Rayner	£2.75
☐ Duncton Wood	William Horwood	£3.50
☐ Aztec	Gary Jennings	£3.95
☐ Colours Aloft	Alexander Kent	£2.95
☐ The Volunteers	Douglas Reeman	£2.75
☐ The Second Lady	Irving Wallace	£2.95
☐ The Assassin	Evelyn Anthony	£2.50
☐ The Pride	Judith Saxton	£2.50
☐ The Lilac Bus	Maeve Binchy	£2.50
☐ Fire in Heaven	Malcolm Bosse	£3.50

Prices and other details are liable to change

ARROW BOOKS, BOOKSERVICE BY POST, PO BOX 29, DOUGLAS, ISLE
OF MAN, BRITISH ISLES

NAME ....

ADDRESS ....

....

....

Please enclose a cheque or postal order made out to Arrow Books Ltd. for the amount
due and allow the following for postage and packing.

U.K. CUSTOMERS: Please allow 22p per book to a maximum of £3.00.

B.F.P.O. & EIRE: Please allow 22p per book to a maximum of £3.00.

OVERSEAS CUSTOMERS: Please allow 22p per book.

Whilst every effort is made to keep prices low it is sometimes necessary to increase cover
prices at short notice. Arrow Books reserve the right to show new retail prices on covers
which may differ from those previously advertised in the text or elsewhere.